About the Author

Rebekah lives in the beautiful south-west of Scotland with her dog, Angel, and enjoys walking around the walking trails, and watching crime TV shows such as *The Mentalist*, *Criminal Minds* and *An Inspector Calls*. After working in childcare and sales, Rebekah decided to finally pursue her real goal, and write a book.

Murder in the Alley

Rebekah Weir

Murder in the Alley

Olympia Publishers
London

www.olympiapublishers.com
OLYMPIA PAPERBACK EDITION

Copyright © Rebekah Weir 2024

The right of Rebekah Weir to be identified as author of
this work has been asserted in accordance with sections 77 and 78
of the Copyright, Designs and Patents Act 1988.

All Rights Reserved

No reproduction, copy or transmission of this publication
may be made without written permission.
No paragraph of this publication may be reproduced,
copied or transmitted save with the written permission of the
publisher, or in accordance with the provisions
of the Copyright Act 1956 (as amended).

Any person who commits any unauthorised act in relation to
this publication may be liable to criminal
prosecution and civil claims for damage.

A CIP catalogue record for this title is
available from the British Library.

ISBN: 978-1-80074-578-0

This is a work of fiction.
Names, characters, places and incidents originate from the writer's
imagination. Any resemblance to actual persons, living or dead, is
purely coincidental.

First Published in 2024

Olympia Publishers
Tallis House
2 Tallis Street
London
EC4Y 0AB

Printed in Great Britain

Acknowledgements

Thank you to my mum, Alison, and my two sisters, Naomi and Esther. Thank you to my cousin, Andy, for helping me navigate the literary world.

Chapter 1

Entering the library and following the gold detail on the stone columns as they stood tall like soldiers either side of the foyer, Helen couldn't help but feel a sense of awe at the craftsmanship. Towering columns of Jerusalem stone birthed into smooth cylinders the size of the trunk of an oak tree.

Her eyes moved up the columns and rested on the high ceilings in the lobby. The pillars reached to the ceiling and stretched to circle the base of the stone domes with glass panels, making the most of the low sun, covering the floor below in maple-coloured light.

Each pillar, painted with shades of blue depicting branches of trees decorated in gold, glinted in the sunlight. Helen followed the detail to the spheres; every little leaf grew from the branches. Today, she had the time to allow herself to become swept up by the beauty she had above her. She would fulfil the house chores and making sure the staff went about their duties in the smoothest way possible, but today she was free from the confines of working for the Ellentons' household.

She smelt the familiar scent of old worn paper, and a sweet warmth filled her nostrils. Helen pulled at the wool surrounding her hands. She rearranged her gloves, stretching her fingers out as the surrounding air went from warm to cool. She heard the hushed chatter of the men around her talking about their businesses with one another and excusing themselves for their tobacco.

The people moving around her focused on only what they needed to do and missed the art that lay above them.

A raised voice came from the check-in desk. Others shook their heads at the noise as they settled back into the books. Helen identified where the noise was coming from, a lady in a burgundy skirt-suit. 'This is a library,' Helen muttered to herself. 'It's where people come for some peace, not a shouting match.'

'I do not believe that I handed in this book late, miss, I should not have to pay for what I think is a clerical error,' the lady exclaimed while making no attempt to lower her tone as she addressed her displeasure at the fee. She paid no attention to the people watching her as she stood at the check-in desk.

Helen noted that all the librarian did in response was to sit further back in her chair and show the lady the relevant paperwork, pointing at something on a clipboard. She didn't seem concerned with the woman who was arguing at her. With her relaxed shoulders and professional smile, the librarian attempted to calm the other lady down. Helen wondered whether it was her training that had allowed her to be calm or was it that she'd done this dance before. The librarian had finished showing the lady the relevant paperwork, after which the lady in the burgundy suit huffed and collected herself, pulling at her clothes.

Helen realised she had stared at the scene. Turning away as a sense of relief washed over her as the library had resumed its normal rhythm, she adjusted her cardigan on her shoulders.

The voice of the lady dimmed as Helen set off to where she wanted to be. However, Helen could tell that she was still arguing the fee. Helen didn't see the lady dropping the matter soon but couldn't help but feel relieved she wasn't in the librarian's place. It must be the worst part of the job, Helen mused, and admired the librarian's patience as Helen went on her way.

Turning her head, curious to see how the argument had ended, Helen watched as the lady stormed out, away from the librarian and down the tiled foyer leading to the street outside. From where Helen stood, she couldn't hear the outside world. The sound didn't travel that far into the building, something that Helen was thankful for.

Helen marvelled at the autumn sun as it beamed through a large floor to ceiling window, setting the gold-painted walls ablaze with colour, making the library feel like a palace of solitude and serenity. Helen knew that this was nothing compared to the sense of calm she would get once she had the book in her hand and sat in her usual spot with it on her lap.

With corridors signposted for the different genres of books they held, leading into rooms with row upon row of books, Helen had walked around this library so many times she didn't need the signs. Her heels joining the noise of shoes clicking gently across the floor. All having a rhythm of their own.

Just as Helen entered the alcove where she knew the book she was looking for would be. an elderly lady approached her.

'Could you help me find this book?' the lady asked. Helen recognised the title as one of the maids at the Ellentons' household liked to read the same genre.

'The book you're looking for is in that section across the foyer, just over there.' Helen pointed at the room where the romance novels were. The woman looked up and followed Helen's finger, then smiled.

'Thank you, miss,' the lady said as she slowly made her

way across the foyer. For a moment, Helen watched her leave, worried about someone so fragile negotiating the traffic in the lobby.

Helen never cared for romance novels, preferring a puzzle to solve. Crime held her attention more; she always had enjoyed this genre, finding out who did the crime, the wild goose chase, the game, and the result of the investigation.

Helen scanned the shelves to find her favourite book. The noise of the library alone was enough for her to become swept away from reality, the books offered her a place to escape to.

Finding her favourite book, *The Complete Adventures of Sherlock Holmes* by Sir Arthur Conan Doyle, was easy. She'd checked it out so many times that she could walk into the library and find it in her sleep. Helen plucked it from the shelf.

Creases revealed themselves in its unstable spine as she took it from its resting place. A small plume of dust billowed in the maple-coloured sun. Helen's fingers stretched; her hand balanced the weight of the book. Helen's lips spread into a smile as the warmth of familiarity filled her. Her hand wiped away the dust that had covered the books either side of it, revealing some on the edges of the old book feeling the thread which made up the title.

Helen felt the warmth of the autumn sun on her back. She tucked the book under her arm and looked for her favourite place to read. She remembered how the armchair that waited for her felt to sit in. How many hours had she spent seated in that same chair? The adventures it took her on, Helen quickened her pace to get there sooner.

The large bay window and the soft leather armchair were strategically placed to optimise light, with a small table near them, piled with newspapers. A cushion lay on its corner against the armrest, looking not too dissimilar to a favourite armchair you'd have at home, welcoming its next visitor.

Lifting her watch, Helen calculated that at this point of the day the library would have very little footfall and so the old armchair would be vacant. The area surrounding it would be quiet, ready for its warmth offered by leather that had become worn down, but the frame on which the leather layover was still solid enough to engulf her. Hence, you weren't at risk of sinking too deep in the chair, meaning you could read for hours and not need to move. The softened leather and the cushion showed it was a much-loved part of the library.

As usual, her favourite chair was in the far corner of the room. Placed with care near the window angled slightly to make use of the light from the window. Helen's cheeks relaxed at the sight of the chair as her shoulders rolled back. She finally slowed down. For nothing could get in her way now. The chair seemed youthful and happy as if it was very content with its place in the world. Feeling as if it was ready to embrace its next visitor. A youthful optimism about the adventures it would take people on.

Folding a newspaper that someone had left open, Helen returned it to the pile of newspapers stacked neatly on the small table. She turned to correct the cushion too. Sitting down, one headline caught Helen's attention. After reading it, another silly caption highlighting the crime spike in the city. Still, the papers had once again overreacted, another journalist wanting to make a name for themselves.

Helen sank into her old friend's arms with anticipation. Settling down and allowing herself to fall into the soft leather upholstery curling her legs under herself, Helen lent against the headrest, lifting the book to her face and letting the cushion support her weight. She began turning the pages of the book, *Scandal in Bohemia*, allowing her to escape into a world of blackmail, intrigue, scandal. She lost all sense of time as she learned about the witty Detective Sherlock Holmes and his loyal friend, Dr Watson.

Her muscles relaxing, opening the book up as she sank deep into the leather chair, the sense of peace and tranquillity took over. Helen read on about the two of them taking on the notorious Irene Adler and sought the clues and facts of the case. As she did so, she felt the temperature drop slightly.

There was a sense of change in the air. Adjusting her cardigan again, she kept her eye on her watch – time had passed quickly. The noise of the footfall disappeared as people came and went. Helen flickered through the rest of the chapter she was on. She'd time to finish this chapter before heading home, she'd still be there before the Ellentons arrived back from their trip out. Helen's role in the Ellentons' house held great responsibility, but came with the privilege, if needed, to delegate jobs to others.

Lifting her head occasionally, pulling herself out of the book, Helen monitored the time of day, her day off would soon be over. Helen didn't need to be back until much later in the afternoon. She took a deep breath, turned the pages of the book, feeling its delicate crisp paper held gently in her hands.

Taking a break from reading as her neck and shoulders ached, rolling her shoulders back, she noticed the time, she needed to think about heading home. Still, a reluctance came over her. She glanced at the book longingly, realising that she had almost finished it. Helen gazed out of the window. The sun had lowered, leaving the street in a half silhouette. She watched as the sun turned the sky from a clear blue to a bright, vibrant orange making the sky look as if it was on fire with hints of pink like that of Turkish delight. Making Helen want to stay. Slipping deeper into her chair, her legs feeling heavy she could feel herself falling asleep with the rest she'd had. Helen reminded herself that there was still a job to do, she could always check the book out of the library another time.

If she stayed for much longer, she'd be cutting it close if she were to get back to the Ellentons' before they arrived home. Helen needed to move and move fast in this case. As she moved, she pondered the classic single phase.

"You see, but you do not observe."

Helen pondered on her favourite phase in the book, Helen's own observation skills were well developed. They allowed her to do her job, as she had a keen eye for detail, a dislike for jobs left undone. Helen had never given them any cause to doubt her integrity.

Helen opened her bag and set about putting her gloves back on, setting her clothes straight before going into the foyer. She would check the book out and finish it when she had the time.

Closing the book shut, Helen untangled her legs and stood herself up. Moving the coffee table back where she had found it, she walked out of the alcove into the lobby that had now dimmed in brightness as the afternoon turned into the dark evening.

Taking the book to the librarian, Helen smiled gently at the young woman who accepted the book from her as she looked at her, checking out the same book for the umpteenth time. Helen suspected they shared their taste in books, and she understood the escape that reading gave Helen.

'This one, again, Miss Squireton, you know there are

other books that are in the same genre?' she asked, not entirely understanding just how much Helen enjoyed the escape this book set offered her.

'Yes, miss, but this is my favourite one, I have read some other crime novels, and they just don't seem to be the same,' Helen replied in a quiet tone, slightly embarrassed at how obvious and predictable she was.

'Are they not intriguing enough for you?' the librarian asked jokily.

'They're just not the same, miss,' Helen replied, laughing at the librarian's joke as she extended her hand to take the book back from her.

'Very well, enjoy your book, miss.' the librarian understood as she stamped the inside page and handed the book back to Helen.

Helen turned and strode off across the foyer and exited the library onto the busy street. She paused on the steps of the building to allow passers-by to carry on with their day, as the smell of car fumes and horse dung hit Helen's nostrils. Helen lowered her head down and lifted the collar of her winter coat up, Helen's eyes watered with the cold Nottingham wind. Helen prepared herself for the winding streets contrasting with the quiet of the library.

There were meals to plan with Miss Henderson, the cook, and the briefing to prepare for tomorrow. Every now and again she got lost in her thoughts as she pulled out and joined the commuters.

As Helen waited, she watched as a variety of people bustled along, from smartly dressed businesspersons to house staff with their baskets and shopping lists in hand. Horse-drawn cabs and carts made their way back and forth on the street, horses' hooves clicking against the cobbled street and the carts bouncing as they pulled alongside them. There was also the odd automobile tooting its horn at unvigilant pedestrians, warning them to get out of the way.

Walking home, Helen noticed the crowd had moved unusually. People were pinning themselves to the walls of buildings or stepping on the road. Helen wondered if this gave her a chance to get home earlier than usual. Straining, Helen could see what all the fuss was about. A stern looking nanny barged through the crowd of commuters with a pram, not too different width of that of the pavement. Helen could tell that this wasn't the first child she'd had in her charge, neither did Helen care for the stout nanny's demeanour. Stepping aside briefly as she walked past Helen could tell she was at the end of her rope, her hat showed signs of regularly being reapplied and her hairpins had broken, loose strands of hair wrapped around them. Commuters filled the pavement behind her just as quickly as they had separated. Muffled whispers to travelling companions filled the air around Helen as they made comments about the brash lady that had just walked by.

Helen reminded herself that it had been raining earlier, so the cobbled stone could be wet, picking her way as not to stand on a loose rock and fall.

Helen breathed steadily as the volume of the streets had made her heart rate climb. Her breathing becoming unpredictable, focusing on her feet and nothing else Helen planned her route home. Keeping her head lowered and her breath steady, Helen slalomed among the other travellers when she saw an opening leading to an alleyway promising a shorter way home.

She watched the opening for a moment, deciding on the course to go. If she stayed on the busy street, Helen knew she would not get home on time before the Ellenton family. The alley route would save her time. However, the alley was dangerous, Helen surmised, built to serve as a link between the businesses and the pubs. It was local knowledge that you use it at your own risk, not a place for a respectable woman. Helen watched the alleyway, thinking about her options. As she did so, a woman, dressed in old threadbare undergarments and a thin shirt with nothing but a shawl over her shoulders, her hair hanging around her in thick, greasy curls, watched Helen while she lurked in the shadows at the entrance to the alleyways. She had noticed Helen's indecision and seemed to dare Helen to take the shortcut through the alley with their damp walls thick with mould and air with the malodour of stale alcohol and sweat; the ground looked uneven with paper bags, stagnant with the fluids in the alley.

Looking back along the pavement, she thought about the noise level of her two options. The original route was long and noisy on her current route home, and Helen was late. However, the alleyways were quicker if not unsanitary. She would have to be careful not to pick up any of the dirt on her shoes or skirt and bring it into the Ellentons' home.

Looking at the alley once again, Helen saw the woman in the alley smile unpleasantly as she turned to enter the alleyway again. Her skirt moved as one piece of rag, solid with the filth of the aisle.

Rolling her eyes at how long she was taking to make this decision, Helen took the risky route home. She was already cutting it close, having to weave between the crowds of people had slowed her down. She would not let herself get sidetracked by the people begging for money.

Helen picked up her skirt slightly higher, she could see her feet better this way, there was no hiding her nose from the smell. Helen tried not to overthink about the mould invading her lungs as she tried not to breathe too much.

Further down, a man in rags slumped against the lamp post.

Helen darted through the alleyways, trying to avoid the unidentifiable detritus on the ground. She marched on, looking neither left nor right. It was a lot more pungent down here in summer, at least in the colder months, it contained slightly less stench.

Helen placed her coat collar over her throat to prevent herself from gagging as the air threatened to seep down her nose and mouth. the thought of the mould engulfing her lungs putrefying the air she breathed made her stomach twist as she thought about the spores from her surroundings inside her. Helen hopped around the bigger, more apparent piles of muck, trying not to let her feet slide out of from underneath her and avoiding the half-drunk men. Helen lifted her head. A gentleman on his way to a pub made his way in the opposite direction to Helen. He'd misjudged how putrid the ground was, after a moment of panic, he regained balance and carried on. Helen refocused on not letting herself do the same.

Avoiding needing to pin herself against the wall to prevent dodging and getting her shoes or her uniform dirty, she heard an unusual shuffling noise, too light a thud to be another wasted man, but also more substantial than a rat.

Helen passed glassy-eyed men, hungover and still drinking, the women, wearing thinning, threadbare clothes, just like their faces, looked at her like a pack of lionesses or vultures eyeing up some easy prey, often turning their bodies, sizing up the way she presented herself. Ignoring them for she had no intention of giving in to the subtle intimidation, a stubbornness took Helen over, she was clearly not dressed like them, and neither was Helen a regular in these parts. Still, she would not feel as though this was their territory and she needed to move along swiftly.

Helen tried not to think about the sinking sound her shoes made as she pushed a loose hair back into its place. Helen walked on, her back straightened. Her shoulders pushed themselves straight, making her seem taller. She could see some other women fade back into the shadows, averting their focus away from her. Helen readied herself for the central part of the alleyway. It would not make her feel as if she needed to hurry along. Helen calculated her route home.

Finally, feeling the stench ease off and hearing sounds of the main street again, she slowly removed the handkerchief from her face. There wasn't much mould left in the air as there was more space for the fresh air to circulate in the bigger alleyways.

Helen stretched her neck out, observing a blonde-haired young woman, well dressed, and hobbling towards her. The young woman was neither dressed for work as Helen was, nor was she wearing clothes like the faded woman Helen saw earlier. She was just dressed oddly, as her outfit was a stark contrast to the alleyway. There was the fact that her hair had clearly at some point been pinned up earlier in the day. Helen looked closer, the young woman was looking around her with eyes wide, every now and again Helen could see her lips quiver giving Helen the impression the young woman didn't understand where she was going, like a lost lamb. Yet, she didn't look as if she was commuting to or from work.

Looking closer, Helen tried to decide whether the young woman was drunk or in need of medical attention. Looking up with panicked sapphire blue eyes, she said, 'Help me, please'

Chapter 2

Realising she did not know how to react to the situation she had in front of her, Helen couldn't help the thoughts spin round her head of all the actions she could take. Helen could run to the woman and offer her help, but in doing so, Helen could slip. They'd both be on the ground before long. Helen could coax the woman to her, but that would take time which neither of them had, or Helen could wait for the woman to get to her. Looking at the state the woman was in, it'll be all over for the young woman before she got to Helen.

Unable to move a muscle, Helen could only watch as the young woman fought to keep upright. Helen watched as the young woman had to bite her lip as she focused on using one leg at a time and having to lean against the wall of the alleyway to support her weight. She watched as the young woman's legs buckled, her hands sinking deep into the green mould on the wall, the young woman tried to stop herself from falling. Pulling her legs in line with her upper body, the young woman's face alternated between scrunched up lips, eyes closed, her eyes becoming full of pain and rapid breathing with the severity of the condition she found herself in.

Helen watched on as the young woman's legs seized, with disbelief, Helen could feel her own eyes widen, anything to stop the scene unfurling before her from happening. Still, Helen found herself unable to do anything.

Helen's eyes locked with the young woman's, her face was as pale as a sheet, and her lips looked like ice. Helen could see that she had no more strength in her.

Helen's arms and feet finally broke free from the freeze. Stepping forward, Helen coaxed the lady to take one more step towards her. Helen would catch this lady, even if she fell herself, not wanting any more harm to come to this poor lady.

To Helen, everything around her from then on felt as if time around them had stopped. Helen's vision from then on blurred everything out apart from the young woman as the young woman fell into Helen's arms. The noise became muffled as the weight and the force of the fall, made Helen's arms ring with the shock of the extra weight. Her own knees bent worryingly. Light blue silk and blonde hair filled Helen's face, staggering as her arms took the impact of the lady's fall at a slightly awkward angle.

Desperately trying to stop the young woman from ending up on the wet ground as not to bang her head, and making things worse for her, Helen's arms wrapped around the young woman's body, raising the young woman's half-dead corpse up off the ground as best she could. Helen struggled to keep the lady in her arms as she tried to adjust her grip on her. Suddenly they both landed on the floor with a thud. The silk clothes kept Helen from keeping a proper hold of her. Helen crouched down on the stagnant earth, next to the young woman.

Helen watched hopelessly, wondering what needed to happen next and asked the young woman the only question on her mind.

'Are you all right?' Helen asked, looking the lady up and down for anything that could tell Helen what was wrong with her. This proved unfruitful all the while Helen remained shocked at this girl's state of health, realising that the young woman was clearly not all right and that the question was, in fact, a stupid one. Still, something about the girl confirmed to Helen that it was the right question to ask. Upon hearing Helen ask this, the young woman's eyes returned to a regular width and her condition allowed her control over her body. It was clear to Helen that all she could do for the time being was to keep this sick lady calm.

For a moment, the young woman looked at Helen with large sapphire blue eyes wide with panic at her own state of health but there was a sense of calm in the young woman at Helen's presence. Then the young woman's head rolled back, and her ailment regained its grip on her. Helen let go of the young woman in her arms, taking in what she saw in front of her. The change in the young woman's health, whatever was ailing her had regained control of her again, and Helen was powerless to help.

The young woman convulsed out of control. Her back arched as her limbs shook, her face distorted painfully, and strangely a smile appeared on the young woman's face, which was disturbing in the extreme. Helplessness filled Helen as she spoke to the young woman. Helen knew there was no one to help her get this woman to safety. Panic-stricken Helen decided it would be a good idea to look for the cause of the woman's ill-health.

As Helen patted the lady's shoulder, she spoke smoothly and calmly. 'It's okay, I'll get you some help,' was all that she could say, on a loop as she got ever more frustrated at the lack of a clue as to what was wrong with the lady in front of her. Helen suspected she also meant it for herself, for there was no way that she could comfortably lift this lady up and carry her to safety, which looked like her only option at this point. Frustration and determination kicked in. There was only one thing clear as day to Helen: the young woman was dying and needed help. Helen would need to find her that help.

Helen's eyes searched for an able-bodied person who looked like Helen could persuade them that the lady on the floor didn't have an adverse reaction to drink. Bouncing from one person's face to another, she hoped to find that someone with more strength who could pick this young woman off the ground, and help Helen get the lady some help, where she could have some safety.

Lifting herself up on to her knees, Helen scoured the crowd looking further into the gathering of people to see those at the rear of the crowd shifting to get a better look. There was clearly no one willing to help. Either not wanting any involvement in what was happening or taking Helen for a fool who couldn't see a severe reaction to drinking too much when she saw one.

Looking back at the lady, now too tired to keep her eyes open for very long and covered in the muck that lay on the floor with her, Helen knew she had no choice. This lady needed help, and Helen was the only person able to give that to her or at least try. Helen thought of ways she could attempt to get the lady to relative safety. Lifting her would not be easy but dragging her was not a good plan, there wasn't much time to dwell on the details. Could Helen take the weight of the lady and assist her walking? Helen saw that taking even more time. The Ellentons were more than likely home and settled by now. Helen needed to be economical if she were to get back at a reasonable hour.

Knowing that it was her duty to do all she could for this Lady, Helen slung her arm around the young woman's waist, resolute that she would get this Lady to safety. Helen half carried; half dragged the young woman back to the busy street.

'Okay, we'll take this step by step, you and me' Helen spoke softly to the woman as she set her over Helen's shoulders and took the first steps, shakily as she found her stride and they moved.

People stepped away from her. Helen continued to carry the young woman. Anger filled Helen. Looking around her at the sombre faces at the scene in front of them, no one offering help. Helen kept going, talking to the lady. Explaining she was going to get help, it would be over soon, one way or another.

The weight of the young woman made Helen less nimble on her feet, nor did she have the energy to hurry as she was forced to put all her strength behind every step. Each time their combined weight made Helen sink deeper into the ground. She despaired at the thought of all the dirt she had on her uniform, the stench she would be surrounded by for the next couple of days.

Helen moved around stagnant bags. The smell bombarding her nose with every step she took. Helen couldn't get to her handkerchief, not without dropping the woman. Helen worked hard to navigate narrower parts of the alleyway.

The young woman's body convulsed violently over Helen's shoulders, causing Helen to tighten her grip on the young woman, so as not to let the young woman fall.

Feeling her own strength all but fail her, Helen's thoughts turned to other ways of helping the young woman. For if she carried on carrying the young woman, they would both be in trouble. Helen could leave her propped up against the wall as she was filthy anyway and get help now, they were closer to the street. There was no guarantee that the woman would be in a saveable condition by the time Helen got back with help. Could the woman wait that long or would fate decide it was her time to leave and her life to end. Could Helen answer her plea. Helen could feel her own bones protest.

'Thank you, I didn't think.' Helen tried to press the woman to finish, but she had lost consciousness again.

Helen shook her slightly, but all the woman said was, 'He would go this far.' Worn out and still no relief in sight, the young woman had gained some level of awareness. Helen's decision was clear, she was to carry the young woman as far as she could and get help.

This could all be in vain, Helen thought as she slowed down to a snail's pace, her legs shaking and her arms desperately trying to keep the young woman up off the ground. But she knew if she were to do her part in helping the poor woman she'd had to keep going.

Finally reaching the busy street, Helen stopped, exhausted by the weight of the young woman and the shock of the afternoon's events. Helen looked around, searching from side to side for help or inspiration. Helen did not know which. Leaning the young woman against her, as she stretched her neck out in pain and exhaustion, trying to stop it from cramping, she heard a voice coming from further down the street.

'Excuse me, miss,' came a call. 'Can I help you?'

Turning clumsily to her right, Helen saw a tall young man making purposeful strides towards her. Taking a deep sigh of relief, her legs let their protest clear at what Helen had just done, for she wouldn't have to wait long before she could offload the young woman. Helen could feel tears fill her eyes at the sight of the young man making his way towards them. Her efforts were not to have been in vain. Keeping the young woman leant against the lamppost, Helen called out.

'This young woman needs help.' Fear and exhaustion covered her words as they echoed down the street.

Letting the young woman gently, slowly, slide off her arm, Helen rolled her eyes in her own relief that she would not have to do any more lifting today. The young man caught up to her and introduced himself.

'I'm Deputy James; I'm off duty, so call me Benjamin,' he said, eager to help Helen and the young woman, calling a cabby to them. The sound of his whistling reverberated off the walls of the houses. He drew the attention of one of the cabbies waiting on the street, waving his arm to make sure the cabby driver saw them, then took the young woman from Helen.

He did not look at Helen until he had hold of the young woman, holding her with ease as the horse and cart pulled up next to them. The speed of the cart forced Helen to take a step back as the cabby's wheel bounced onto the pavement. A whoosh of air circled them as the cabby came to a halt next to them.

Helen could feel a wave of something come over her. It wasn't dizziness, shock. Helen had the horrid thought that she may faint with all the effort.

Deciding that it would not happen, Helen blinked a few times as she watched as Benjamin helped them both.

Helen noticed the way he clambered into the cab with ease, carrying the young woman. Helen watched as he placed the young woman on a seat in a manner one would settle a baby in a cot, with one hand at the back of the woman, his arm under her shoulders. The other was under her knees as he bent to enter the cab and sat the woman down on a seat furthest from the door. That way no one could see the woman was in trouble. Helen guessed that this was to maintain some level of the woman's dignity.

Once in the cab, Benjamin took his coat off and wrapped it around the young woman. Helen got into the cab herself just as the cabby set off at speed for the hospital. Deputy James helped Helen balance as she went to sit next to the young woman wrapped in Benjamin's coat. Helen hoped to help the young woman to remain in her seat.

Benjamin smiled gently at her, revealing a set of perfectly straight teeth. Helen could see kindness in his dark green eyes, set in a paling complexion as if he had been outside regularly during the warmer months and now that they had gone, so had the colour from his skin.

Once Helen was comfortable in her seat, Benjamin sat in his place. She noticed the lack of distinctive lines in his shirt, even with his sleeves rolled up. As he reached across the young woman, preventing her from sliding off her seat, Helen noticed a slight rim of paler skin around his watch.

Looking at the young woman sat opposite her, they weren't too dissimilar in age or stature. The young woman was more youthful and prettier than her. Still, Helen couldn't shake the feeling that the two of them were alike. Helen remembered seeing her in the Locus Nectar a few times, and the young woman had a sort of warmth to her. Now all she felt was cold, as whatever was ailing her relinquished, and regained control of the young woman, taking her on a horrid ride as it tried to take the young woman's life.

Speeding towards the hospital, the young woman's

gasping became worse, as the seizure continued to grip the young woman's body, taking it for all the fight she had in her to breathe as she was now barely able to stay on the seat. Both Deputy James and Helen mirrored each other's concern. Both of them looked at each other, their eyes broad, neither of them wanting to breathe as the breath left the woman's body. Time had a cold frost to it for a moment. After a minute of nothing but the cabby's whip cracking was heard, Deputy James reached out to hold the young woman's hand, as Helen suppressed a tear and looked outside the window, covering her quivering lip with her hand.

Clasping the woman's hand in his, this seemed to console the woman. Watching him do this, Helen flashed back to how the punters watched the young woman as she sat, chatted and drank. On occasions, she'd sing along to a song coming over the radio, or if a tune came into her head, she would sing that too. Helen remembered the bar seemed warmer and brighter when the young woman was in. Helen couldn't help but think that the world would lose a little of its vibrancy should this young woman die tonight as she refocused her mind on something else. She continued watching the world go by at speed. Everything had stopped for the victim. It seemed too surreal to be real. Sure, people die every day, but not like this. Helen remembered the panic the woman had shown on her face and the few moments of calm. They were both stuck in the alley without help when the ailment had relinquished control momentarily.

Watching the grey that had engulfed the world, Helen couldn't help but feeling as though everything had slowed down. This part of the woman's life had not ended well for her. The cold, exhausted feeling inside Helen, making Helen want to shiver, mirrored the world outside as it wrapped around Helen's body, squeezing tight. A tear rolled down her cheek, and Helen herself had no energy to fight the cold.

The young woman's battle with her condition ended in the cab as her lungs made a gargling noise, her lungs emptied its last breath. Whatever made her like this had relinquished its control of the young woman as her body finally gave up the fight for life.

Limbs became soft and doll-like, no longer able to hold its own weight. Eyes became glassy as the young victim's lips grew pale as the young woman's own body heat left the body. The young woman's form collapsed in on itself, falling against the wall of the cab. Helen wondered whether her effort was, in fact, in vain.

Deputy James took a mental note. He looked over at Helen, sympathy written all over his face. She was a civilian and had no training or experience in dealing with dead bodies looking back at her. Shock. The woman was dead.

Her hands flew to her face, she tried to hide the tears from him, not wanting him to see her while she was in such a state as her back arched, and her chest felt tight with grief. After the moment of initial shock, relief and grief passed Helen looked out the window. Helen told herself, even though it's silly, she couldn't help feeling a little responsible for the victim's death. If she'd taken her to safety sooner, then maybe there would've been time to take her to the hospital alive instead of the police station, dead.

'Was she a friend of yours, miss?' Deputy James asked in a soft tone, reaching out for her hand, trying to read what Helen's state of mind was. Could she be left alone or were there two people that needed his attention?

'No, I don't know her, Benjamin,' Helen replied, slightly weepy. After a pause, Helen answered his question again. 'Actually, Benjamin, I have seen her before, at a bar I frequent occasionally.'

A wave of guilt filled Helen as her hands shook. Stretching them out in front of her, Helen scowled at this lack of composure, and shook her hands, followed by placing them either side of her, hoping he hadn't seen them shake.

'We're going to drop the body off at the police station where our pathologist will aim to find any next of kin as the hospital can't do anything for her now,' Deputy James explained as he tried to console the now grieving and in shock Helen. Benjamin paused regularly to maintain some eye contact with her, asking her if she was all right occasionally.

'Are you sure you're okay to do this with me, miss?' Benjamin asked Helen, taking in Helen looking dishevelled, her uniform all mucky. He showed the same level of concern for Helen as he did for the victim.

'I'm guessing you must ask me questions once we get to the station, Benjamin?' Helen replied. Benjamin nodded. 'In that case, I'm fine, I'd rather do it this way than have to take more time out of work so soon after my day off.' Benjamin nodded and turned his attention to the dead body once again.

It became apparent to Helen that this was not Benjamin's favourite part of the job. He began shuffling uncomfortably, keeping a distance from the dead body. 'Then we must go round the corner, to the station where my superior, Detective Arthur, will have questions for you.' At this point dismay washed over his face, knowing the extensive questioning she would be in for, questioning himself on whether she'd be up to the task.

They pulled into the side entrance to the station. Along the outside wall of the building sat a police wagon, dark wood with iron bars across windows barely the width of a child. Breathing deeply, slowly, Helen readied herself, just in case.

Deputy James clicked open the cab door. As he jumped out, he explained what was going to happen and what Helen was to expect. 'I don't think you want any more surprises,' he spoke as he turned to face her. Helen shook her head.

Deputy James lifted the dead woman out of the cab, with the help of a policeman standing at the door.

Twisting to face Helen slightly, he said, 'You'd better stay here.' Pausing slightly, Deputy James thought this could be too much for her. 'But if you'd rather wait and go home, I can arrange for you to come in tomorrow.' Deputy James offered to take her home himself if that was what she wanted to do.

'I need to do this now, Deputy James. The young woman needs me to do this now,' Helen replied, pulling at her dress and shifting from side to side with anxiety. Deputy James went into the room and logged in the dead body. Chemicals wafted into the corridor. After a moment he came back to collect her and walk Helen back around to the police station, always keeping one eye on the road and one eye on Helen.

Helen felt numb. She couldn't make sense of what'd happened. She was desperately late for the Ellentons.' Hoping this wouldn't result in her losing her job.

If it did, over something like being late, Helen would struggle to get another job. She'd have to start all over again to earn the new family's trust. It would ruin her reputation.

'Who do you work for, miss?' Deputy James asked. 'Would you like me to send one of the junior officers to explain what's happened?'

Helen thought about this for a moment. This would buy her time and would fix the problem of her being late. But somehow, Helen didn't feel as if she wanted the help. She was so lost in her thoughts. Helen couldn't think of anything other than the alleyways and the young woman as she staggered towards her. Just a few moments ago. 'No, Deputy James, I'll be fine,' Helen replied wistfully.

Helen took in the change in Deputy James's demeanour as she replied a little puzzled why she didn't want him to offer some respite and avoid her getting fired from her job. 'Do you see me as a suspect, Deputy?' Helen asked.

Deputy James took a moment. 'Personally, no I don't, you still must answer questions like a suspect,' Deputy James said, apologetic at the way the day had gone for Helen. 'My superior, Detective Arthur, will sort this out. I'm sorry you saw the young woman taken into the autopsy room.' Deputy James explained that ordinarily, he wouldn't ask a civilian to do that, but he needed to monitor her as she was the last person to see the young woman alive.

Benjamin showed the way back out of the side building. 'We'll go out and around to get to the station. This way,' Benjamin said as Helen followed him.

Feeling a little emotional at the evening's events, even Helen's breathing was shaky as she found a seat in an office that Deputy James had pointed to. Turning her head, looking out of the station window as people on the street rushed by, ribbons of grey and black painted the canvas of the window, the street lights a splash of vibrancy in a grey background.

Watching Deputy James tend to the victim, Helen couldn't help feeling as though she needed to explain why she was the one dragging the half-dead victim out of the alley and onto the street, where he'd found them. What made her offer help rather than walking away like everybody else?

'Deputy James, she needed help, and she wasn't dead. I thought she'd just need help to get home, I thought I could bring her here while she was alive and then leave her here. I was trying to help,' Helen said too quickly, struggling to make sense of the situation she was in.

Helen remembered how the victim's silk dress felt as it picked up the muck off the floor like a sponge mopping up water.

'It's okay, miss, you did the right thing, I'm just sorry you had to see all this, you'll now have to answer some questions, and that's not pleasant, that's all, miss. I'm worried you're not up to it today, but the fresher the memories, the clearer the details,' Benjamin replied softly.

'I'm not a suspect.' Helen finished her explanation, hoping Benjamin would see the situation when he saw her and the young woman coming out of the alley for what it was, not murder, but someone trying to help someone in crisis.

'You still must go over this, in the station, I can't write you off as a suspect just because you say you're not. You understand, don't you, but I can say that you want to come back to the station another time for questioning once you've recovered? Would that be preferable, miss.' Benjamin paused, as he realised, he didn't know Helen's name.

'Miss Squireton, and no, I'm fine to do this now, Deputy James,' Helen replied, now looking at her hands, red with the effort of carrying the young woman. Her bones once again protested, and her legs ached, as images of people moving out her way, resurfaced. Still, not one person offered her any help, finally, relieved of being able to hand the young woman over to Deputy James.

Feeling hopeless as she pulled a handkerchief out of her satchel. Wiping away as many of her tears as she could, as they flowed down her cheeks, she made no noise, just wiped the tears away, being too tired to do anything else.

Her body ached every time she remembered what she had done that day. How it started off so well, the library, her book. The leather chair. And now Helen was in the police station being questioned about an event she had nothing to do with other than being civil.

Chapter 3

Looking around the station from where Deputy James had left her to gather up the relevant paperwork, Helen got the impression it wasn't much like the entrance of an old bar, with its dark wooden reception desk and muggy white painted walls. The air felt icy. Helen didn't quite know whether that was just her reacting to the shock of what had happened, and finally beginning to understand that she was now safe. The young woman was where she needed to be or whether it was cold in the station, the entire building was mostly made of stone, punctuated by beams on the ceiling, and around the door frames of the offices.

Dim lamplight made the station look warm, but the lack of heat contrasted the aesthetics of the building, only vaguely hiding that this wasn't a place you wanted to spend your Friday evening. The décor failed to conceal the true nature of the building.

Helen couldn't help but rub her hands up and down her forearms as her legs shook again. All Helen wanted was her bed. Still, she knew that if she were to postpone this to the morning, Helen might never want to come back. The quicker Helen could answer the questions, the faster she could get to bed and leave this ugly chapter behind her.

The main reception area was large and unforgiving, then there were a couple of offices, each one made of wood, dark and beaten. The structure had clearly been there for a while.

Helen wrapped her shawl tighter around herself as her lips quivered. Helen's eyes closed tightly, trying to avoid crying in Deputy James's office. However, her attempt was trivial, as still a tear rolled down her cheek. Her skin had become sensitive with the constant wiping away of tears. All the while, other police officers and civilians bustled past her, not noticing she was sat in Deputy James's office. Acute shock made her feel like ice, tears sliding down her face as she stared into space in disbelief that they had classed her as a suspect. She was here to contest her innocence.

Hearing a loud bang and the sound of keys in a lock, Helen spun around and looked out into the station reception area and saw Deputy James receive some paperwork and a light brown case folder from the officer at reception, then make his way over to her.

Helen saw Deputy James turn to face her from a filing cabinet, as he put the paperwork, he'd taken out of the filing cabinet into the case folder. Quickly, she wiped her face, feeling the smoothness of her hand against her cheek before Deputy James could notice she had been tearful.

Finally settling down, Deputy James took his own seat in the chair on the opposite side of the desk to Helen, with paperwork and a pen in his hand.

'I know a lot of this already, Miss Squireton. Now we must follow procedure.' Deputy James paused as if to gauge Helen's response. Helen hoped he wasn't looking too closely as she could feel her eyelashes were still wet with tears. Watching as she moved her hands along her eyes, she would not give him another reason to suggest that they do this in the morning.

After a moment of awkwardness continued, 'To make

sure we catch who did this to the young woman and to see if this is in fact, a murder, and the criminal gets caught, we need to do that within procedural actions, so it doesn't get laughed out of court.' Helen watched as he changed from a caring young gentleman to a professional police officer. 'This also allows us to go through things in more detail, so we have a better understanding of what happened,' Deputy James explained to her.

'I understand, Deputy James,' Helen replied, the shock causing her tone to sound cold as her heart rate increased, making it hard for Helen to talk without being in pain. She bowed her head as she realised how her words had come across, then raised her head again, readying herself to relive the evening's events.

'Let's start off with you running through your day before crossing paths with the young woman,' Benjamin questioned her.

'It was my day off so, after morning briefing and finishing some jobs off in the morning, I had gone to the library to read a book, I helped an elderly lady look for a book, I mean to say I pointed her in the right direction of the genre of the book. I almost bumped into some gentlemen conversing about something political. Then I went to find the book I had read. I had a seat where I could look out of the window as I read, then when it was time to finish, I left.' Helen paused.

'And what time was this?' Benjamin asked after he had finished writing what she had said.

'About six o'clock,' Helen replied. Benjamin nodded.

As she answered his questions, Helen couldn't help but notice he was still in his civilian clothes. Not even a hat or a different shirt had been put over his everyday clothes as he diligently jotted down Helen's answers on the paperwork. Helen recalled the day's event and wondered what went so horribly wrong for the now-dead young woman. How strong she must have been to get herself somewhere she could get help. Even if the young woman didn't make it all the way, the young woman had her wits about her, even in such a state that she could take herself away from whatever bad situation she was in and go in the general direction of where help may be. How fortunate for the young woman that Helen was there to help her. Judging by the reaction of the bystanders and the folk around while Helen was helping the young woman, there would've been no help for her if Helen had set off from the library a few moments earlier. 'All it took was a few minutes,' Helen spoke out loud, not realising she was still in conversation with Deputy James about the incident.

'Sorry, miss, can you repeat that?' Deputy James asked, bringing Helen out of her trance.

'I'm sorry I was only thinking about how it was a matter of a few minutes between me bumping into her or not. Had I left earlier, then I'd never had seen her.' Benjamin nodded and continued taking notes.

'If you can, Miss Squireton, can you tell me if there was anyone about acting suspiciously, a little too eager to watch you and the young woman in the alley maybe and maybe a description. If you can't then don't worry,' Benjamin asked professionally, but with an element of softness to his voice.

Helen began running through the faces she had seen while on the floor with the young woman as she was trying to call for help. Feeling the shock of the event crawl up her body, Helen took a deep breath before answering.

'To be honest, Deputy James, the whole crowd looked a

little over interested, like they were at some freak show, but no one stood out as suspicious, no,' Helen replied while she continued to run through the faces in the crowd. Again, Benjamin nodded as he jotted this all down.

'And you carried her through the shortcut, where I found you carrying her into the street. Did you get help from anyone while you were there?' Benjamin asked.

'No, Deputy, I called out for help, but no one came to help until you saw us on the street near the lamp post at about six-fifteen.' There was a moment of silence as they both paused, Benjamin looking through his notes for another question to ask.

Just then, a middle-aged man with a weathered face barged into the room. The smell of tobacco seemed to linger on his clothes. He was heavier on his feet than the lanky Deputy. This led Helen to believe that the older, heavier set gentleman, must be his superior, Detective Arthur. Deputy James sat up straight and then got up and went to the middle-aged man.

Cold air encased who Helen suspected was the Detective. As he turned to close the door behind him some cold air wafted towards Helen pinching at the side of her face and down her body. Fighting off a shudder, Helen shrunk away from the cold as it tried to nip at her skin. Even though she had wrapped her cardigan around herself, something about the Detective drew the warmth out of her.

'This is the woman who came in with me,' Deputy James paused, taking in the Detective's confusion about why Helen was in the Deputy's office, but shortly after continued to explain. 'A young woman died with no sign of a weapon, sir. I thought at least it needs an equivocal death investigation. We also need to see if she's got any family, sir. Someone will have to notify next of kin,' Deputy James interjected as he handed the paperwork in its folder to the other gentleman. By the tone Benjamin used when he talked to the older gentleman, Helen figured that the older gentleman was most definitely Detective Arthur.

There was an uncomfortably long silence, as Detective Arthur took an unnecessarily long time to go through the paperwork. Helen could hear him thinking something over as the paper cracked as the Detective was going through it with a fine-tooth comb. Neither of the men exchanged words while the Detective looked the paperwork over. Helen was feeling uneasy at what had taken the Detective's interest. When finally, Detective Arthur spoke, with a low voice that matched the weathered face he wore.

'Thank you, Miss Squireton, you can get on with your evening now,' Detective Arthur said as he handed Deputy James the paperwork back to file it away. 'Deputy James and I will take it from here.'

Taken aback by his cold dismissal of her, telling her to leave without so much as an acknowledgement at the sheer effort it was both emotionally and physically to make sure the young woman got the help she needed. Helen had not been raised to make such a cold dismissal as just the way things were. She remembered her father saying, 'It doesn't matter what gender you are, you are human nonetheless, and deserve respect.'

She understood she was no longer required, and that there was nothing more for her to do, but Helen felt a little put out at the lack of sincerity in his comment.

The contrast between him and Deputy James had hit

Helen like a brick – one lanky, young, and compassionate, the other older, more substantial than Deputy James and as blunt as a stone. Helen wondered whether that made working together easier or was there going to be a clash of personalities.

When she didn't leave straight away, both police officers looked at her, bemusement clear on their faces, and Helen wondered what to do next, her eyes switching between the two of them. She did not want to leave until she had confirmation that they would take this seriously.

Helen glanced at the two of them. While Detective Arthur had dismissed doing anything about the case put before him, Deputy James seemed to agree with Helen. As far as they both could see, there was something suspicious about the young woman's death. He met Helen's gaze, and there was something in them that suggested to Helen that he would have liked to pursue the case of the victim's death.

Empathy for Helen washed over his face as he switched his eyes between her and Detective Arthur. Likewise, Deputy James looked as if he was looking to the Detective for his orders, on whether to take the case.

But Detective Arthur just dismissed both Helen and the investigation, handing the paperwork down on the Deputy's desk like it was just another batch of paperwork he would have to file at another point. But neither did she wish to outstay her welcome. Not wanting her stubbornness misconstrued as selfishness by Detective Arthur or Deputy James, Helen thought better of it not to press for an apology for the Detectives' judgement as the Detective looked over the paperwork that she and Deputy James had worked through again. However, she couldn't help herself asking to be let in on information about the case.

'May I know of the progress you gentleman make?' Helen

asked, knowing that the answer from Detective Arthur would be a no. Still, Deputy James may be persuaded to keep her informed. There was already a clear desire to go further with the case in Deputy James, and it would be a matter of convincing him to go behind Detective Arthur's back.

Concerned by the lack of interest by Detective Arthur, she did not want to leave without knowing that the young woman's death would have an investigation. For there'd been a sharp drop in the amount of police time dedicated to deaths in the alleyways. Helen knew that as there were often crimes down the alleys and the unsavoury characters that lurked there meant the police no longer dedicated so much time and resources to policing them. She was slightly aware that she may have asked too much.

'Why would you need to know such a thing, Miss Squireton?' Detective Arthur's puzzled tone matched the look on both the men's faces, but he continued to explain, 'You've done your bit, Miss Squireton.'

'I would like to know when you catch the murderer,' Helen replied, stating the straightforward answer for wanting to know the progress of the investigation. After pausing and seeing that this wasn't helping her win the argument, she continued to explain her request by saying, 'I knew of the young woman, Detective, regardless she died at her prime of life, and while under my care. There's something about how the young woman acted while I began assessing the situation before I carried her to the street where Deputy James saw us. The young woman had been panicking, like the young woman knew she was dying.'

Helen could see a little shift in weight from both of them, seeing that they had made a little more sense of the situation

Helen carried on. 'So, I would like to know that you've brought her a little justice.' Playing the damsel in distress, Helen shuffled her weight from side to side as her blood boiled at what she had to do to get the two men in front of her to heed what she was saying. They were just wasting time, the time needed to catch the victim's assailant. As she knew full well, that she was anything but a damsel in distress.

'You'll find out in the papers, like everyone else, if we are successful in solving the case, Miss Squireton,' Detective Arthur said with a tone as icy as the northern wind. 'There is no need for you to jump the queue and get any privileges because you're the one who brought her in.' He dismissed her again, this time not even looking at her as he turned to face the door, planning to leave, to have the last word.

After a while, Detective Arthur looked at Helen, as if he was measuring or calculating his next move. Helen fluttered between feeling uneasy about Detective Arthur's unwavering gaze on her and a feeling of defiance. Helen thought he'd thought better of his blatant dismissal of her. He launched his last assault. 'You're a civilian, Miss Squireton, with no investigative training. There is no need for you to be kept abreast of the case,' Detective Arthur stated with a sense of cold release, as he turned and walked away.

Chapter 4

'Excuse me, sir, but I was in the cab with Miss Squireton,' Deputy James paused, his face softened, looking to the side. Helen could tell he was calculating something; he clearly didn't question Detective Arthur regularly. 'She may not be law enforcement, but she is a witness. It might serve us well to have her alongside us.' Calming himself, stepping back from Detective Arthur, Deputy James' face turned to that of a watchful one. He seemed to look for some clue as to how his superior had taken his actions. 'She has seen the victim occasionally so, if ever there was a person we would need to speak to, without delay, Miss Squireton would be that person, sir. I have my doubts about how much cooperation we would have at this hour of the evening, sir, if we wait till morning, it'll be even harder to prove that the woman died either of her own actions or murder. The case would go cold either way,' Deputy James suggested as his chest widened.

Helen observed Detective Arthur as he reacted to this. It was clear to Helen that this wasn't usually how things worked between Detective Arthur and Deputy James, particularly because Deputy James was quick to back down after he made his initial point. Helen wondered why such a display was uncommon between them, for she knew Deputy James to be capable. Still, somehow when Detective Arthur was near, there seemed more than professional capability being questioned.

This puzzle hadn't left her mind as she watched the two men read each other like books, that was, until one of them spoke.

'She cannot understand the ways things get done, Deputy James. You'd do right not to forget your place,' Detective Arthur retorted indignantly. Detective Arthur seemed to think that Deputy James had spoken out of turn, Helen didn't think so. As far as she could see, he was offering a different option, not questioning his superior. Either way, Detective Arthur didn't like it.

'Sir, with all due respect if she can be head housekeeper of the Ellentons' house, who we know are from good stock,' Deputy James argued. 'Then why do you think her incapable of understanding the investigation process?'

Detective Arthur paused for a little, then tilted his head as if he'd just thought of another jab he could take. Helen steadied herself, questioning who this attack was for. Detective Arthur knew Deputy James had a point, being head of house meant Helen was a capable young woman so could understand how an investigation worked. Helen was about to find out who Detective Arthur's next target would be.

Detective Arthur turned towards her as she remained seated, growing tired of the conversation and Detective Arthur's pride impeding getting a young woman some justice.

'Why would you want to worry yourself about such things?' A little concerned at Helen's interest in the case and a little deflated, he continued to apprehend the reason for Helen wanting to be informed of the progress of the case. 'You didn't know the victim well, so why all the interested in this case? It won't change my mind,' Detective Arthur added as he took Deputy James' seat and leant back nonchalantly. 'Rather, help me understand your persistence in knowing how the case progresses.'

Helen noted that Deputy James shifted his weight, uncomfortable at the Detective sitting in his seat. Detective Arthur clearly had an issue with being questioned. Helen couldn't help but feel that there was more to it than that. The Detective had already made it clear where the Deputy's place was. What was the need for such an action?

His eyes scrutinised Helen, not letting her escape his gaze, watching her reaction to every second of the conversation that enthralled them. Neither one losing face. Helen thought this was a silly, time-wasting game of wits when a murderer was on the loose.

Feeling frustrated at the lack of compliance displayed by Detective Arthur, it wouldn't hurt him just to say yes. Helen knew she would have to be careful how she answered so as not to draw attention to her state of mind. Helen needed to keep her head on straight if she were to win this mind game. Realising that her heart rate was still high, and that she hadn't yet fully recovered from the emotional turmoil she had just been through, she reminded herself that the more of her actual state she showed, the more grounds Detective Arthur would have to dismiss her in a way that soon would not be correct. What with the stirrings of civil unrest of the women's rights movement, Helen calculated an appropriate response expecting Detective Arthur's next move in this mind game he had locked her in.

'No, I don't know the victim well, Detective,' Helen began answering his question, breathing deeply for a moment, putting her frustration at the interrogation aside while she argued her point. Helen could see that Detective Arthur would not take this decision lightly, there was more persuading to be done. Deputy James stood listening intently, like a spectator to a sport. 'However, as I've already explained to the Deputy here. I've seen her in a bar I frequent every now and again.' She looked towards Deputy James, who stood a little straighter beside the Detective at the mention of his name, almost standing to attention. Observing the two of them as they went back and forth, Helen wondered about his view on this. 'I only wish to know whether you'll take the case seriously and not let her death get swept under the rug. The way she looked as I bumped into her didn't seem to me as the way a young lady would look if she was in that state willingly.'

Seeing that this was not winning either of them over, Helen continued to argue her case. 'With all the bloodshed recently in the Great War, I can't have this girl dying, despite Deputy James's and my best efforts to get her help, on my conscience.' Helen reminded Detective Arthur that the country was still licking its wounds. 'Do you think after what all our young men have gone through, coming home to find that the police had turned their backs on those who they'd gone to war to protect, they would be happy with your actions? I may only be a woman to you. However, to the young woman, who is now in a morgue, I was her last hope.'

Letting her breath slow down while remaining upright with her back straight, Helen waited for Detective Arthur to respond. Noticing out of the corner of her eye that Deputy James had smiled, it was only at the edges of his mouth. But there was definitely a smile invading his lips, his eyes glistened in the lamplight, for a moment it was all Helen could do was to stare into his eyes.

Once Helen knew she was staring at him, she shifted her weight a little. Regaining some focus, Helen wondered for a moment what it was Deputy James had found amusing. She was merely arguing her point. This wasn't a comedy show, and he knew it, then she turned her attention back to Detective Arthur.

Seeing that there was still a little way to go until Detective Arthur was convinced to let her into the investigation, Helen made her last plea to any better nature that the Detective had in him, tired and as worn out as he looked. Surely there was some decency left in the man sitting before her. Was he really willing to let a woman's death go unsolved as the price for keeping face. The case goes cold, and the lady's body is left to be a nameless body, a victim unidentified, and dying without justice? Helen hoped and prayed that it wouldn't end like that.

'This girl died in agony. There's got to be something suspicious about that, while it's true people die every day, people don't die in agony every day.' Stopping herself from identifying the fact that people mostly die in their sleep, and that was most definitely, not the case. 'If this Lady was a young gentleman, or if I were a man, you wouldn't dismiss the case or me so quickly. Would you, Detective?' Helen argued back. A wave of anger at Detective Arthur's continued dismissal of her on the grounds of being a woman rose in Helen as she waited for a counterattack.

The Detective sighed and seemed to have shrunk into himself. Not wanting to admit anything to Helen either way, his weathered face twisted as he realised that this Miss Squireton would not let this lie and leave it be. She would become a pest which, if not watched, could lead to the investigation being void.

'All right then, we will keep you informed, Miss Squireton, but only if it doesn't interfere with the case,' Detective Arthur warned with a growl. Helen had done it, albeit by twisting the Detective's arm, she had got him to agree to her at least being informed on the case and had made an allied force in Deputy James, but she had a feeling this was not the end of the war.

'Of course, Detective, I wouldn't want to interfere with a man's job.' Helen didn't quite know whether she was taking one last jab at Detective Arthur or stating that she understood, but she knew one thing: this is precisely what she will do, well to them anyway.

'I'll let you know if I hear anything further.' Helen shouted back, happy that she had won the debate and content because she could now ensure the young woman was going to have her justice. There was no reply. Helen fancied that Detective Arthur was not up for arguing with her on that point. For Helen reckoned, he now knew better than to draw swords with her.

Helen was not about to let the young woman's death go unpunished. Helen pondered on what the woman had said to her, "I didn't think... go this far." There was a person or persons unaccounted for in this chapter of the woman's life that Helen was now a part of, her picture was incomplete, and she hated it. Helen poured over her journey with the young woman on her back, thinking about how the crowd had reacted, asking herself the same question Benjamin had asked about the crowd. Could Helen have missed someone? Was whoever going "this far" as the woman had put it, only minutes after bumping into Helen? Helen's keen sense of justice took over, filling her with a sense of duty that she must ensure Detective Arthur took on the case. It was up to her to make sure that the lady's death was taken seriously. Helen worried over there being a killer on the loose, she didn't want any of the maids, who were the same age, if not younger than the young woman, falling foul of the same fate.

Pushing open the grand door of the Ellentons' house with her arm, her face contorted as her elbow joint clicked with the force it needed. On any other day Helen could have opened it with ease, but not this time. This time she needed to put all her body weight behind it. Placing her shoulder near the handle, Helen pushed hard, bending her back a little as she did so and shuffling her feet. The door finally moved, slowly, as Helen had to stop and take a breath before opening the door any further.

Quietly slipping into the large reception area, Helen stepped into the main hallway as the tile floor gleamed in the moonlight from being freshly polished earlier that evening, relieved that, even in her absence the other staff members had no qualms about what it was she expected on her return.

Worried that her lack of timing was felt by now, as this wasn't a common occurrence, she crossed the grand entrance hall; she noticed the entrance to the drawing room was ajar, and it looked like only a lamp was on.

'Helen, is that you? Would you mind coming in here, please?' came the deep, tired voice of Mr Ellenton.

'Yes, sir,' Helen replied. Helen could feel her heart become heavy as it seemed to sink into her stomach. She lifted her head to the sky, taking a moment to despair quietly at how her day had started off so well, only for it to end with one unfortunate event after another. Then, pulling her cardigan over her chest, she strode towards the entrance to the lounge.

The lounge door was a little lighter than that of the entrance door, making Helen push a little too hard. This caused Helen to stumble a little with the force she had used, her legs felt a sharp pain as she increased her grip on the doorknob, refusing to let the door fly open and knock the lamp on its post near the entrance to the room. Sliding through the door and seeing that both Mr and Mrs Ellenton were present, Helen wondered if there was a more serious reason for her being summoned. She started analysing all her actions that week that may be the reason for her being summoned other than her uncharacteristic tardiness. Helen couldn't think of anything but would soon be at ease.

The room comprised dark wood furniture with deep red carpets and heavy curtains, as there was not much room for change after the Great War. The entire country faced a time of recovery, and that was clear in this room of the Ellentons' house. There was also an air of not wanting to change, to keep things as they were, for Mrs Ellenton had lost a younger brother in the war, some of the staff too, hadn't come back from battle.

'Sir, is there something I can do for you?' Helen asked once she had closed the door behind her, taking in the room again, checking if it had been done to her standards. The room had clearly been polished, and the carpets felt smooth and clean. Relieved that it would not need to address it in the briefing, so there was only the one staff member she would need to speak to, Helen concentrated on Mr Ellenton.

Mrs Ellenton sat on the sofa in a lovely lilac chiffon dress, with Mr Ellenton's Nottingham lace trim around her neckline, and some lace gloves. Her caring nature matched Mrs Ellenton's outfit, it was as feminine as she was. Mr Ellenton was still dressed in the clothes he was in at work that morning with a similar design pocket square. Helen presumed that he'd got in from work only recently. She had noted that there were recent tire tracks out on the driveway from Mr Ellenton's car, the house was in the country suburbs of Nottingham, far away enough so it was a quiet estate but close enough to town, making it easier for Mr Ellenton.

'Care to explain why you're in late, Helen?' Mr Ellenton asked in a firm but light tone as he swirled his whiskey around his glass gently.

Helen tried to gain composure, for this conversation was to be about her tardiness, something she knew the Ellentons were quite clear about, that their staff should never make a habit of being late. Helen moved her eyes to the ceiling, for she knew crying would not help the young woman, or her answer Mr Ellenton.

'Sorry, sir, but a young woman I was helping had died this evening while under my care.' Pausing, and realising that she needed to explain further how she had come to be helping the young woman who had been in her care. 'I bumped into her, and as she was unwell, I stayed with her until a very nice young police officer offered his help.' Helen paused; Helen's brain flew images of the young woman convulsing out of control around her head. Feeling a lump in her throat, Helen was quick to swallow and let her eyes blink away the rising tides behind her eyes, trying hard to regain some composure. After a moment, Helen continued with her explanation as to why she was not back earlier.

'I had to assist, as the witness, in processing the death both at the morgue and the police station,' Helen continued.

'Oh, my dear, are you all right after all that?' Mrs Ellenton said sympathetically. Almost jumping out of her seat to hug Helen but thought better of it and shifted her weight in her chair, for however much Mrs Ellenton was a kind-hearted lady,

Helen was a staff member not one of the ladies she had over for tea.

'Will you be needed any further as they launch their inquiry into the young woman's death, Miss Squireton?' Mr Ellenton asked, even though his tone was very business-like, Helen could tell he was speaking softly, he only meant to make sure she had the time she needed to be helpful to the police.

Relieved after the day she'd had, she could still keep her heart at its normal rhythm, but she was tired at the day's events and frustrated that she was now stood in front of her employers. She felt as if the spotlight was on her. Her temperature rising now as she needed to give herself the flexibility to pursue the case. Helen couldn't admit that she had taken on the case herself, especially as it would be behind the Detective's back. She would need to lie to him for her to give herself an alibi to do her duty to the young woman. She had built up such a stable professional relationship with them, now she risked throwing that away. Feeling uncomfortable about the risk, Helen reminded herself that the young woman needed her to do this.

'Possibly, sir.'

'Very well, let us know how we can support you and the police in this matter, if needed,' Mr Ellenton said kindly, smiling slightly as he tilted his head towards the door behind Helen, excusing her to go upstairs.

Helen curtsied quickly and made her way to her room. Her knees ached with a throbbing pain as she tried to keep her arms and hands from shaking from the strain of the evening. She walked slowly up the stairs as she massaged her arms.

Helen found herself once again remembering the severity of her situation. She didn't know who the killer was, or even where they were at the time the young woman had fallen into her arms. Helen remembered how vulnerable they both were. If someone had murdered the young woman, then there was no guarantee that either of them were safe as they sat in the alleyway while Helen thought of what to do next; the murderer could have been nearby. How easy it would have been for the murderer to take advantage of the two of them being in such a state. She could have ended up their second victim. A wave of fear and frustration came over Helen.

Twisting her neck slightly, she'd noticed that a crevice in one statue wasn't glistening in the moonlight as it should. Stopping to inspect the figure further and looking closely at the icon, her back ached at taking the weight of even her own body and it was proving troublesome. Helen began noticing that one of the house staff had neglected to dust the decorative piece on the stairwell and tutted. She felt the dread of how her muscles would ache in the morning, and her early start.

Once in her room she got dressed, slowly. She slid her nightwear over her head and unpinned her hair. She glanced at the single picture she possessed, a photo of her family: her father, mother, and both older and younger brothers. Feeling the loss of members of her family to history, she breathed slowly, in and out. Helen took a moment to relax her thoughts before continuing to move through her bedtime routine.

Pouring the warm water into her washbasin, left for her by the scullery maid, the transparent crisp noise the water made as it tumbled and swirled around in the basin allowed her heart rate to calm. Her muscles relaxed. Helen breathed, feeling the steam settle on her face, then drip back into the bowl, as she looked at her face in the mirror. Nothing but the sound of her breathing and the gentle dripping of the water dripping back into the basin.

Glimpsing herself, Helen's brown locks had loosened around her shoulders, her green eyes still puffy from the strain of the day. Sighing and furrowing her brow at how untidy she must have looked to the Ellentons, as she washed her face, Helen could only imagine how much of a mess she must have looked to the two men. Frustrated that both Detective Arthur and Deputy James had seen her in such a state.

Setting about sorting herself out, reflecting on how Deputy James had stuck up for her in the confrontation between her and Detective Arthur, Helen remembered how Deputy James had taken her side over Detective Arthur. Clearly, a risky move between them. Knowing the mess she was in, Helen couldn't help but think there was a possibility that it was because he saw Helen as vulnerable, someone needing protecting. Or was it that Deputy James agreed with Helen that there should be an investigation into the young woman's death? Helen thought that if Deputy James' motivation was the latter, then maybe there was change coming, it wasn't just hot air that things were changing, and this also meant that she could call on him if she needed help with pursuing the case. But Helen wasn't sure either way.

A pang of frustration hit her in the stomach as the realisation dawned, that Benjamin may have seen a vulnerable woman. Helen's annoyance only grew when she realised how all of this could have given Detective Arthur more reason to disallow her to "help" the investigation into the young woman's death. Even if it were to only be an equivocal death investigation. Playing back in her head what she had said about the country still reeling from the Great War, Helen kicked herself for giving such a low blow to Detective Arthur. It was not her most distinguishing moment. She looked at herself again as she picked up her face towel to wipe her face.

Once Helen had dried off her face, her need for rest overcame her. Throwing her cloth in the basin's direction, barely looking in the direction she wanted it to go, it flopped over the edge allowing most of the fabric to be on the outside. Helen watched as it slid with a bump off the bowl and fell with a thud onto the floor.

Glaring at it before rolling her eyes as she picked it up and put it in its correct place, Helen's knees threatened to give in. Helen placed her hand on the edge of the table with the basin on to steady herself. Feeling the weight of the towel, Helen folded it properly, feeling its warmth and softness in her hands, then carefully placed it on the rack. Then she settled herself in bed, whispering to herself, 'Tomorrow's another day.'

Getting up as the cold first sunlight glistened through her window, Helen stretched every joint she could while lying in the warmth of her bed.

Placing herself at her desk to write in her diary, slowly as her arms and legs stiffened uncomfortably, remembering the pain from the night before and calming herself from the shock. Helen reflected on what a day she had, the young woman who had died.

Helen remembered a few times when she was out at the bar when the entire population of the bar would gather around her as she sat or stood at her favourite spot. All you would hear was the young woman's voice but could seldom see her for her entourage. Her bubbly, warm, confident life had ended in fear, agony, and squalor.

It was time to get started finding out how this young woman died before the demands of her day job took precedence, Helen pulled out a few pieces of paper from a drawer and a pencil from a pencil holder, she started taking notes on what she already knew.

Helen knew the young woman to be a regular at the Locus Nectar. She found it frustrating that the young woman's life was so free and careless when once upon a time a girl her age would do needlework indoors and host tea parties, rather than drinking and being the apple of any man's eye in the pub. Helen wrote a preliminary timeline of events as she saw them.

Helen knew it was on Friday 10, September at about six o'clock that she saw the young woman coming towards her in a well-used alleyway that Helen was using to get home to the Ellentons quicker, to avoid not being late. Given the later hour of the day and that the woman wasn't wearing working clothes, Helen suspected she may well have been heading away from the bar when Helen found her. It then took Helen about two or three minutes to realise that the woman needed help and to take her out of the shortcut and to get the woman to safety. Then finally being seen by Deputy James on the main street on the other end of the shortcut, for the woman to die in the cab at about six thirty.

This led Helen to wonder how such a woman came to be in that position. Would she ask for help if she had felt like she had drunk too much, or given her constant attention, would someone not suggest she go home and sleep it off? This didn't seem likely to Helen, as the men were mostly too drunk to notice that the victim was awfully ill. Therefore, the young woman knew she was in trouble rather than just needing air to sober up.

Helen cast her mind to what the reason behind her death could have been.

Taking in the memory of how the young woman looked, Helen wondered how whoever had put the woman in such a state had done so. How the convulsions had engulfed the young woman. Helen thought about the possibility of a grand mal seizure. Was it a case that the person knew of the woman's underlining health condition and took advantage of that when trying to kill her? The young woman was aware of what had happened to her. Was the young woman looking to go to the hospital herself, if so, why didn't the young woman just ask the bartender to call an ambulance? Undoubtedly, the young woman knew better to make her own way there. Confusion on the events leading to the young woman entering Helen's life filled Helen. She had so many questions that needed answering if she was going to get justice for the victim.

Helen also thought about the possibility of a heart attack. Helen noted the young woman didn't at any point clutch her chest. Neither did a heart attack measure up with convulsions still, Helen knew that if it were a simple seizure, you'd be more likely to die through asphyxia or exhaustion. She remembered picking up a few basic forms of medical knowledge from her father's books when she would sneakily read his medical journals and dictionaries. Nothing seemed to add up in her mind, albeit she was no expert.

Helen remembered keeping an eye out for any injuries while she had the young woman in her arms and then on her back. There was no injury visible, they were all internal injuries. Seeing how hopeless the situation was, Helen believed that this was going to be all in vain, she wasn't a police officer, this was going to go nowhere.

Sitting back in her chair, Helen thought about the fact that she was not the police. The police did investigations. She should just give up, do what Detective Arthur had told her to do in the first place and leave it to them to solve. Then Helen thought of the fear the victim showed, how violently the young woman had died, things were changing, the old attitudes were being questioned, why shouldn't Helen help the police with their enquiries? Why should Helen sit and wait for them to do their job? Helen breathed in slowly, straightening herself up. She tried to remember the finer details of the incident.

There was a slight scent of alcohol on the victim, the scent suggesting she was in a bar but didn't smell the way one would if you had a significant amount of alcohol and she dressed formally rather than for a night out. Helen was now beginning to pace up and down her room, stopping, she took a breath and tried to steady herself, looking at her thoughts again with a little less emotion. There was no sign of drunkenness, this ruled out death via natural causes. Pausing for a moment, and sighing, feeling annoyed at how little she had to go on considering that she was there when the young woman's condition deteriorated, weighing up what options were left if you ruled out the possibility of death through natural causes. Was there a chance that the woman was a victim of an attack or beating? She was so filthy at the time Helen had looked for signs of what had happened to her, and Helen was in shock, could she had missed something in her panic.

Reflecting on her own state of mind and the woman's condition, Helen's eyes tightened at the thought she could have missed any signs the woman may have been beaten, realising that the muck from the floor would have hidden any bruising or lesions on the woman's skin. Helen continued to weed out the possibilities of what killed the young woman, continuing with the ever more likely idea that the woman could have been beaten.

If she'd been beaten, there would be bruises. Where were they on her body? Helen thought long and hard about how many other ways someone could kill their victim while leaving minimal trace of the offender ever having touched or been near the victim. Helen couldn't escape the fact there was a lack of any physical evidence, as far as she could see at least. Then Helen came up with the idea that you don't always have to kill someone from the outside, it's possible to kill from inside out.

    Helen's lips pressed together with the thought that it was possible she was looking at the cause of death the wrong way. Which meant the probable cause of death could have been poison, poison being the easiest way to kill someone from the inside out, leaving little evidence on the body, if any. Plus, there's the fact that unless you knew you were looking for poison in the victim's body, you'd never find it. Helen's eyes lit up as she came round to this being a more viable cause of death. It seemed more workable than being beaten, matching it up with what Deputy James and herself saw when the victim was in her care. Helen ran through all the potentially lethal substances she knew of, beginning with arsenic, but quickly ruled it out as that leaves a foamy residue on the victim's mouth, none of which was on Helen's victim. Noting this all down, Helen finished and got changed from her nightwear to her uniform.

    Settling into the daily chores, Helen made a mental list of the things she had to do for the day ahead; she would need to talk with the house cleaner about the dusting If she allowed it to go further It would make the house look dull and not the shining grandeur that it was. Allowing her time to herself before getting provisions for the kitchen, she planned her day further, as she put the finishing touches to the list of jobs she needed to delegate to the other staff members for the day. Helen thought she might squeeze in some time to go to the

Locus Nectar and enquire where the young woman worked to see if she could piece together who this girl was outside of the Locus Nectar.

She wondered what she hoped to achieve in going to the station after. Was she going to gloat to Detective Arthur about the fact that she was right about the young woman's death? That's if they'd realised that there was something suspicious about the woman's death, or was it purely to ensure whether they'd taken the case on? To find out if she'd been played or not.

Judging by the lack of interest in her being involved with the case, Helen thought twice about going into the station with nothing to offer. Still, she could enquire after the victim at the Locus Nectar in the morning when the bartender would clear away the debris from the night before. Thinking she could count on her already having a friendship with the bartender there, Helen hoped she could gather some more information about the young woman that the bartender might think twice about handing over to the two police officers.

Satisfied with her plan for the day, Helen refocused on setting about who was to do what with Mr Benton and then continued her day doing her chores.

Chapter 5

Helen finished morning briefing by laying out that there were extra chores to be done as the Ellenton's were expecting company who were staying for a few days and that she would go into town to order the extra food needed for the extra mouths to feed.

She watched Miss Henderson's reaction change to that of reserved panic to relief that Helen would be the one to do the extra footwork needed.

This meant that Helen could gather the relevant information to look at the case properly. She knew she could not rush gathering the evidence. There was no point in doing this in haste, for if she missed something, or messed the investigation up some other way, the young woman would not get her justice. Detective Arthur would most definitely not reopen the case if it all fell apart; even if someone opened the case, the evidence would've been ruined, and no longer valid. The young woman's death would forever remain a cold case.

Helen knew if she were to do this behind Detective Arthur's back, she would need to bring Deputy James alongside her. A pang of guilt filled her. Could she persuade him to go against his supervisor? Could she handle the consequences of him doing so? Detective Arthur had already warned him about stepping out of line. This could cost Deputy James his job. Helen couldn't see any other way of going about it while ensuring that any evidence she found remained valid, costing the young woman her justice.

Helen knew that if it got back to Detective Arthur, it would most definitely result in her being kicked out of the case. At least there was a chance that Deputy James could be persuaded to reopen the case on his own, and then Helen's goal would still be achieved. It may have to be without her, that would mean that the young woman could never get her justice. There was no guarantee that by the time the case got going the evidence would still be there. Would Deputy James risk his career over taking sides with her and not his superior? Taking a deep breath, she began to imagine Deputy James losing his job over her and the case, sure it would be his decision. Still, if she'd had a hand in him losing his job, it would be her fault. Would she be able to carry that with her on her conscience? Was it worth making him lose his job?

With tightening muscles, her jaw had pulled itself into a stern expression that could cut through ice, she rolled her head to relieve the tension in her neck. She decided she would solve the case herself, even if she were only a woman in the Detective's eyes, it was her duty and hers alone.

Helen kept her head down and diligently went about completing her tasks for the morning thoroughly and quickly to allow herself time to do what she needed to do in her lunch hour. She had noticed the other maid whom she needed to have a word with, about the lack of proper care and attention the stairway in the reception had, like herself, an unusually busy morning ahead of her.

She felt that pulling the maid out of her morning routine to talk to her, wouldn't be wise. Putting them both behind schedule would only mean more of a rush to get things done, and Helen knew that was when jobs didn't get done correctly, that would also postpone her ability to get started on the case.

Finishing the discussion she was having with Miss Henderson about any changes to the meals they'd planned, Helen found that this had a calming effect on the plump looking cook, she saw that the delivery truck had gone, she'd have to walk on foot into town.

First, she made her way to the Locus Nectar, where she knew she could get a better idea of this young woman's character. Planning her thoughts as she went, ready for when she would speak to the bartender, this time going a long way round as to make sure there would be no more surprises lying in wait for her that day.

With her legs still sensitive from the night before, Helen's progress on the walk was longer than usual as her legs continued to feel fragile. Ignoring it, Helen knew that if she stopped for too long, then the pain would become worse. Her legs would seize. Plus, she had the promise of a seat at the bar.

Pushing the bar door open, Helen's nostrils were greeted with the familiar smell of yeast and other base ingredients fermenting the surrounding room. Helen didn't find it unpleasant, in fact, she thought it matched the feel of the place well.

With the door closing behind her, Helen looked at the old dark wood furniture, with coloured red crushed velvet seats softening the metal bronze detail. They had placed the bar stools in their places earlier that day. Helen felt a sigh of relief come over her as her legs longed for the comfort of sitting near the bar would give her. There was also the practicality of not needing to make it into a big song and dance about the young woman dying, especially as Helen's involvement in the case was questionable at the very least.

Lifting his head up as the bar door hit the bronze bell that was mounted on a block of wood near the entrance chimed, highlighting that someone had entered, Henry questioned her. 'You know we're not open to customers, don't you, Helen?'

Wondering whether he was joking or whether he was seriously suggesting she wanted a drink at this early hour of the day, she smiled sweetly, then realising what he had asked, Helen double took at him, matching his initial confusion. After a moment of silence, Helen explained her purpose for being at the bar so early in the day, and that it wasn't for her own means other than to ask him whether he could help with a personal enquiry she needed to make.

'I'll help in whichever way I can, Helen, what do you want help with?' Henry smiled in his usual bubbly way, as he organised the clean glasses out of the sink and placed them on a tea towel, which he had laid on the countertop. Then, with the tea towel he had hanging over the waist strap of his apron, he cleaned each one individually and placed them by the countertop without a cloth.

Looking away for a moment, wondering how to proceed. Helen knew she needed to be careful not to alert anyone to why she was asking after the young woman. Neither did she want to give too much away at this early stage of her investigation. There was also the fact that if this got back to Detective Arthur or Deputy James knew of what she was doing under their noses. Helen decided on an alibi to enquire after the young woman.

'You don't know where I can find the young woman who I've seen in here often, blonde and quite exuberant, shall we say.' Helen paused for a moment, reading Henry's reaction.

Still, all he kept doing was cleaning the glasses. His face was almost expressionless. 'I'm wondering where to find her.' Helen paused for another moment as Henry seemed to have become puzzled at Helen's need to find her. 'There's an opening in the Ellenton house for a post she may be interested in.' Helen probed gently, not wanting to alert Henry to what had happened to the young woman, for she did not yet have any suspects. By default, Henry should be the last person who saw the young woman alive. For sure, neither did she want to extrapolate anything until she knew more about the victim and her character.

'I'm guessing you mean, Grace. I don't think she'll be interested as she's Mr Hexham's secretary. Grace is paid well I believe, by the amount of money she has handed over for drinks,' he replied while indicating with a nod of the head towards the cashier and struggling with his plumb fingers to get to the bottom of the glass he was cleaning.

Helen gently took the drink and the towel from him, smiling a gentle smile, for she knew she could polish and clean the glass better, and with her dainty fingers she cleaned the bottom of the glass. As she passed them both back to him asking, 'You wouldn't know if she was here last night, would you?' Helen paused. 'Only if she was, and it's the weekend I may find her somewhere else, other than here, do you know where she would go?'

Henry shook his head. 'I wasn't here last night, and I don't know where she goes when she leaves here. I presume to her apartment.'

This sounded like an unlikely answer as she knew for a fact that Henry made sure he was on shift on a Friday as that was the busiest time of the week. On a rare evening Helen was in the bar, and it was busy, Henry would make sure he had extra hands behind the bar, but he would always be there. Henry wanted to make sure they were doing things the way he wanted them done.

The use of his language always puzzled Helen, and she realised it again, apartment, not flat. Helen thought Henry was English. Still, a large part of his vocabulary comprised American colloquialisms, Helen wondered why that was but thought better of asking as she didn't want to sound rude.

'Are you sure Grace works at Hexham's Solicitors, Henry?' Helen asked, as that would mean she could have come from the bar or work when Helen found her.

Henry shrugged his shoulders. 'That's what she told me, 'He replied, getting even grumpier at Helen. Helen put together a timeline from when Grace died, her presumed hours working, and time it would take to go from work at Mr Hexham's to the Locus Nectar. This would give her a time to ask about should anybody else need to be asked about Grace's death.

She knew it was the closest bar to the solicitors by a long stretch, and that Grace frequented the Locus Nectar regularly, meaning that the bar that was easiest to get to and from on an evening without Grace getting into trouble on her way home would be the Locus Nectar. There were plenty of alleyways and pedestrianised parts of Nottingham that would offer shortcuts from Mr Hexham's solicitors to the Locus Nectar that Grace could have taken. Helen knew the alley where Helen had bumped into Grace was the only shortcut leading to the main street. Thus, the closest to the police station. If Grace was trying to get to the station, this would mean she knew she was in trouble, more than the usual intoxication. Helen's heart sank at the realisation of the immense fear Grace must have felt when she knew something had gone wrong.

Based on Helen's musings, she knew she needed to consolidate her theory surrounding the timeline leading to Grace's death. Taking a deep breath, Helen surmised that there were two ways she could do this. One way she could do that meant she could consolidate her theory on her own, however, this would not go down well with Detective Arthur. Was Helen willing to jeopardise her involvement in the case?

That meant the second option. This could provoke Detective Arthur to stonewall her and freeze her out of the case. This would mean that she wasn't doing anything behind the police's back, nor was it impeding the investigation, as Detective Arthur so clearly highlighted his concern with what she was doing in no uncertain terms. Helen wondered if she were to go with option two, how much proof of wrongdoing Detective Arthur would have to stand on if he were to accuse her of obstruction of justice and tampering with the investigation. If she had enlisted their help in going along with her plan, either way, she knew Detective Arthur would not be happy with her.

Helen weighed up the two options for a while. She knew her timeline was all but theory and so not admissible evidence of what happened when and where, other than the secondary crime scene where Grace had fallen into Helen's arms. Deciding to go with option two, Helen knew she would have to tread carefully. Letting Detective Arthur and Deputy James tag along in what was actually her investigation would mean staying within police protocol. Thus, Helen could not use her credibility and standing in the local community, to help her get answers to the questions.

Now convinced option two was still the best option,

despite having to play by someone else's rule book. Helen planned how she would go about getting their attention and convincing them to go along with her plan of how to consolidate her timeline from circumstantial to undeniable.

Chapter 6

Glancing at her watch, Helen needed to leave the Locus Nectar to go to the solicitor's, to see if she could develop a better account of Grace's character, rather than make assumptions based on the tiny amount Helen knew of her. Helen also needed to inform Mr Hexham of Grace's death, that could go some way to making sure that Grace's death did not go unsolved. Even if it were a heart attack or liver failure, they would still need to rule out foul play.

Informing Mr Hexham of Grace's death served two purposes. The first, was that through informing him first, Helen would have the upper hand in ensuring she wasn't frozen out of the case. For she'd earnt Mr Hexham's favour. This put outside pressure on Detective Arthur, other than the pressure he could get from Deputy James, to pursue the case and not let it go cold. Grace was more likely to get her justice. Mr Hexham had no such loyalty to Detective Arthur as Deputy James had. Having two people who knew Grace know and confirm that it was the same Grace meant that there was a minimal chance of mistaking the woman who was lying in the morgue.

This increased Helen's resolve to prove him wrong. She could solve this case, not only that, but she could also do it without Detective Arthur's help. All she needed to do is get enough people to see that she was intelligent enough, and then

Detective Arthur would have no choice than to let her continue.

If Helen had a male comrade who was able and willing to apply pressure on Detective Arthur to keep the investigation going, it could mean that Helen would have more movability to go about getting Grace her justice without having to be careful about it getting back to Detective Arthur.

Leaving the Locus Nectar, Helen thanked Henry for his help, pushing her coat tight around her body as another cold bluster of wind rushed by. An odd sense of heaviness came over Helen. What would happen if all this work would go nowhere. Helen knew that just because you catch someone doesn't always mean they get the sentence they should, evidence can be hidden and falsified. Then her hard work would be out the window, and she would be made a laughingstock. Taking a deep breath as the solicitor was in sight. Thinking about whether she was ready to plan how she would react if it didn't go to court, Helen couldn't help but feel that all she needed to do was try. Making it to court, she couldn't help with that, but at least there would be an investigation.

Seeing the large corner building, standing tall with a rounded overhang from the roof where a stone engraving showed that this was the place Helen was looking for. The stone comprised a pleasant blend of cream and light brown. It was clear someone had taken great care in building this building; cool tones offered a pop of colour in the grey scene that gave the other buildings and the sky above her an odd calmness washed over Helen.

Failing to open the wooden door, Helen tried again, needing to put all her strength behind her and press her entire body on the door to fight a bluster of wind that had caught Helen of her guard. Helen entered the solicitors.

A chill ran through Helen as she noted the delicate nature of what she was going to address Mr Hexham on. That being the dead young woman was an employee of his. There was the feeling of uncertainty about how to encourage Mr Hexham to recount Grace's character allowing Helen to get a better picture of how Grace got into the state Deputy James and Helen found her in. Then there was the confirmation that he had employed her. Maybe he knew about any next of kin that needed to notify about her passing, leading to Helen having an accurate source of information about her character, who she was. Whether any of what Helen had seen of Grace's state was normal. Also, they could confirm if Grace had any medical issues that, if mixed with alcohol, could cause such a reaction.

Standing to welcome Helen was a tall, chirpy young woman, younger perhaps than Grace, but not by much. 'Can I help you?' she asked with a gentle but confident manner. The receptionist was similar in stature to Grace; blonde locks were pinned neatly in an up-do style.

'I'm looking for Mr Hexham,' Helen replied as she closed the door against the wind and took a seat. 'I have a rather important matter to discuss with him.' Taking in the sounds and smells she had around her, like the sounds and smells of the library. There was the sound of tapping fingers and the high-pitched noise of the typewriter needing to be pushed back, followed by more typing.

'One moment please,' the receptionist said, as she made her way down the narrow corridor. While she waited, Helen looked around again. There were filing cabinets next to her, organised in alphabetical order. Some labels were fraying, with ink fading, needing replaced, and Helen followed the cracks of paint revealing the silver of the metal underneath.

A little while later the receptionist reappeared with an elderly-looking man with salt and pepper hair, round glasses in a stylish office suit, with a slightly pale-looking face, in contrast with his intensely blue eyes, following the receptionist down a narrow corridor barely one person wide. Helen presumed was Mr Hexham.

'Madam, you wanted to see me?' he asked, with a head tilt at Helen.

'You must be Mr Hexham.' Helen smiled as she raised herself off the seat and shook his hand with a firm grip. 'I'm Helen Squireton. I've some information to share with you.'

Opening the door for her and standing to one side, Mr Hexham stretched out his arm into his office and stood to wait for Helen to enter.

Once inside the office, Helen noticed another room just across the hallway, with a lady in it tapping away at her typewriter. The lady had stiffened her jaw at the sight of Helen. Lifting her eyes away from her desk for a moment, she glared through the glass at her, making Helen's spine tingle slightly as her blood ran cold.

Turning her attention to the office, Helen could see the office also had space for another secretary. Everything was in neat piles, and light brown folders were stacked with dates on. Helen could vaguely make out that each one had a date, and what Helen only assumed was a case number. There was no paper in the typewriter. The room itself had little light in it, it felt cold, and not helped by the fact the filing cabinets were black and metal. Mr Hexham brought Helen's attention back to him, coughing sharply, then pressed Helen to continue into his office.

'I'm here to enquire about a young woman that I believe goes by the name of Grace Andrews,' Helen continued once settled in his office, sitting herself down on the chair on the right side of his desk. Placing her bag on her knee, she said, 'I'm led to believe she works for you, is that right?' hoping in equal parts she was wrong and right. If Helen was misinformed, then that meant that there needed to be another look into Grace's last movements before she was found dying by Helen in the side street.

Noting the considerable time that had passed since Grace's death occurred and the effect it would have on the case, this gave plenty of time for the perpetrator to think of an alibi or even skip town, never to be heard of again. Helen knew she needed to tread carefully now, so not to put her foot in it with Mr Hexham or Detective Arthur.

Watching him close the door behind her and smiled at her, a kind of bitter smile, Helen got the impression that both Henry at the bar and Mr Hexham may have something to hide. Never a good sign. Helen observed Mr Hexham twisting the doorknob to make sure he shut the door properly. Helen wondered what she would do if her plan of merely asking questions went south. There were people around, but people hadn't shown themselves to be helpful to her recently.

Mr Hexham straightened his posture, trying to make himself more prominent and more threatening as Helen gave in to her impulse to correct a slightly tilted pencil on Mr Hexham's desk. There was a shuffling noise coming from Mr Hexham as Helen moved his pen, Helen removed her hand from his supplies as Mr Hexham replied to Helen's enquiry.

'What about her?' Mr Hexham asked, sharply.

Helen was busy checking for any other items that needed

adjusting, Helen noted that on the shelves were small pellets of rat poison, focusing on the pallets, she was too busy to sugar coat what she was about to say. 'She was found dead in one of the alleyways near the Locus Nectar a few days ago, Mr Hexham.' Regret instantly filled Helen, as she closed her eyes and kicked herself over the lack of sensitivity in her voice.

Mr Hexham's extreme reaction to an employee no longer being alive almost made Helen do away with any thought that Mr Hexham had anything to do with Grace's murder at all. He became small and quiet for a moment and then sobbed, puzzling Helen. Not a reaction of a professional business owner hearing of his employee's death. However, there was a chance that it could all be an attempt to throw Helen off track. One thing was for sure, his reaction wasn't professional, or at least what Helen would describe as professional.

With his face in his hands, he shrunk in size almost immediately, barely making it to his chair. Once he had, using his desk to keep him from falling, he collapsed into the chair, causing it to lean back slightly. He whispered, 'Oh, my dear, dear Grace.' With grief more than one would expect from an employer. 'What happened?' Mr Hexham asked after he had regained some composure.

Helen took a breath, wanting to be as delicate with Mr Hexham as possible after the blunt and abrasive way of giving him the news of her death and hoping that he wouldn't overthink the fact that she wasn't with the police and report back to Detective Arthur. This would put doubt on any evidence she may have found and costing Grace her justice. 'That's what I'm here to find out, I'm taking it she worked for you?' Helen asked gently. Mr Hexham nodded once, then pulled himself together again.

'Is there anything else you need from me, Miss Squireton?' he asked between sharp breaths.

She considered Mr Hexham's feelings on the matter for a moment. 'Yes, Mr Hexham, I'm deeply sorry for your loss, but I have a few more questions. Was she at work on Friday just gone, the 10th?' Helen asked, endeavouring to be as sensitive as she could be. Mr Hexham nodded and tried to steady his breathing. 'How was she, did she seem all right in herself I mean?' Helen asked, watching Mr Hexham for signs she was pushing things a little too far.

'She seemed a little distracted and asked to leave work about five minutes early. She said she was dealing with some stuff in her personal life, I didn't press her on the matter, but I allowed her to leave early. There wasn't a lot to do, and I had planned to stay a little later, anyway,' Mr Hexham replied. It had become clear to Helen that Mr Hexham was in a sensitive state, she thought better of asking any more questions.

Doing so might risk Helen being found out by the police and becoming a suspect herself. 'Thank you, Mr Hexham, I'll take my leave of you now, I know where to find you if I need anything else from you.' Mr Hexham tilted his head towards her in acknowledgement.

Helen excused herself and exited the solicitors to order provisions for the kitchen. She would head to the market to consider and ponder what she had seen earlier that morning. She nodded goodbye to the receptionist and pushed the door open. Once again, the bell chimed as the door knocked it gently.

Chapter 7

The market wasn't that far away from the solicitors. Still, Helen's legs wrenched with pain, as she hadn't taken enough time with doing her chores she'd planned to that morning. Helen's mind focused on doing enough chores to allow her time to get started on gathering information on the case, not thinking that in doing this, she was making things worse for herself. She needed to clarify exactly where Grace was coming from when she'd bumped into Helen. With knees clicking with every step she took, Helen argued with herself, as she pushed on to the market until it came into view.

Making her way closer to the market, Helen heard the shouts of the market stall owners and the horses whinnying in response to the noise and clicking their hooves. Getting closer, Helen could see the bottleneck entrance used by the merchants' carts. Next to that, was the slightly wider pedestrian entrance to the market. Breathing a sigh of relief, she watched the traffic ease as she came closer. This meant Helen didn't need to elbow her way through the entrance, she knew that today neither her mind nor body could take that much exertion.

Once in the market, Helen set about gathering the right ingredients on the list she had made for Miss Henderson that morning. Picking up one fruit, and checking the quality of the ingredients, placing them in her basket with care, making sure that she didn't bruise any of the softer fruit.

Helen inhaled the market air. The scent of sweet fruit filled the air as she moved from stall to stall, Grace and the case never being far from her thoughts.

Nothing about this made any sense to her. Replaying the first time she had seen Grace she couldn't make heads nor tails of where she was coming from. Both the Locus Nectar and the solicitors were in the same part of town so Grace could have been coming from either location. Still, then the time of day and the way she was dressed showed she'd most probably be coming from the Locus Nectar. That fitted in with what Helen knew. This led Helen to think about both Henry, the bartender, and Mr Hexham's reactions to her enquiries. Surely Henry didn't know she was dead. However, there was a question of why he'd become defensive with Helen. Then there was Mr Hexham's reaction, which was all over the shop, from overwhelming grief to that of a defensive response and back again, neither of them a correct response in their given situations.

Moving to a stall with a wide variety of vegetables, again touching the food that took her interest, she tested them for ripeness, for she wanted the ones with the most shelf life in them to allow for the kitchen to get through them before they went off and had to be chucked out.

'Is it the right time of year for celeriac yet, sir?' Helen asked the stall keeper as he lifted some more vegetables into the display.

The stall keeper smiled. 'Not yet, miss, you're looking for celeriac in December to early March miss.'

Helen had got to know most of the stall keepers during her time at the Ellentons' house, though she would never call them by their first names. Even if she weren't in the house doing chores, she was still at work, and in her uniform.

Helen smiled and nodded at the stall keeper, then she rustled around in her bag until she found the backup meal ideas and placed that order. Knowing the family would still enjoy what she had planned.

Helen used her experience and expertise developed through her service in the Ellentons' house to change the relevant ingredients she'd need for the backup meal ideas. She knew that the children liked their eggs runny in the morning, so they could make as much mess as they could annoy the nanny. Both Mr and Mrs Ellenton preferred theirs harder for the opposite reason, Helen had surmised.

Still feeling the aches and pains of not really taking it steadily since the incident in the alley, as she went about her chores, Helen longed for her bed. As she began making her way through the streets quickly, for if she slowed down, she would almost stop. Helen informed the stall owner to send the bill to the Ellentons' house and made her way back to the Ellentons' kitchen.

Finally, in the kitchen, Helen called over a foreman and gave her basket to him. 'Could you give this to the cook? Help her put it all in the right place please.' With a nod, he took the basket from her. Helen made her way to the significantly sized chalkboard used to keep track of all the chores, sighing in relief she was done for the evening, twisting her neck to relieve some tension as she moved up a flight of stairs into her room.

Helen's need for rest overruled any sense of dignity as she unpinned her otherwise neat hair. Not caring that there was male staff about, she practically slammed the door, leaning against it as she pulled out the last pin. Helen needed to empty her mind of all the day's events, as she did often. She did so while barely keeping her eyes open as she scribbled the recent information in her diary, the events of the day.

Pulling her chair back as she steadied herself by her desk, Helen tried to slide herself gently into her chair. She seemed to just land in her chair; her legs giving up on carrying her anymore, Helen twisted her neck and rolled her shoulders, ready to make an account of the day, as she did most days.

Barely able to keep her eyes open, today's entry would need to be a quick one. Her mind whirled with the day's events. If she were to fall asleep now, she would not rest but merely be in a dormant state all night, only to wake up the next morning stiff, sore, and unable to do tomorrow's chores to the standards that she would expect them to be done by anybody else.

Picking up her pencil, Helen noticed how violently and painfully her hand shook, her grip was weak. Breathing slowly to steady herself, she wrote in her journal how the day proceeded on a path she had not expected. Describing the physical demands of carrying Grace Andrews's almost dead body through the alleys and catching the attention of Deputy James.

Pausing for a moment, she leant back as a wave of anger came over her at the way Detective Arthur had treated her. She decided, that for the moment, to skip that part, as making an account of that would open a Pandora's box. She would spend all night writing about his mistreatment of her. After she had finished, Helen finally settled into bed, closed her eyes, and drifted off to sleep.

As she did so, images surfaced of Grace becoming cold as ice, while her body lost all will to stay alive as death encased her body. Deputy James holding her and laying her in the cab, Detective Arthur's discrimination of Helen. She couldn't help herself but shiver in her bed as she tossed herself from left to right as she avoided the onslaught of unpleasant images flying around in her mind.

Chapter 8

The next day, Helen and the other staff members sat at the sizeable pale-coloured wood table. The difference between seasoned servicemen and women compared to the new staff could not be more visible. Newcomers struggled with the mornings. Staff who'd served longer ate, enjoying the ambience of the room.

The warmth of the kitchen only encouraged people to fall back to sleep once they had finished their food. Helen's eyes ambled while she ate her portion of stodgy porridge with the smallest amount of sugar. The room filled with hushed tones of acknowledgement of each other, filling the air with a sleepy sense of appetites being filled ready for the day ahead. The noise of spoons against bowls, almost rhythmic, offered a steady flow of non-intrusive noise in the background of hushed tones.

Helen's eyes rested on Dolly, the house cleaner Helen wanted to talk to, so emptied her bowl.

'Dolly, I have something to discuss with you today, would you mind following me into Mr Benton's office?' Helen requested then turning to face Mr Benton. 'If you don't mind us using the office for a moment, Mr Benton.' Not giving him much choice.

Mr Benton nodded, for his duties for the day required him to be elsewhere, so he was not using the office until later in the day.

An air of dreaded silence rolled over the table, and some female members of staff lowered their heads, like school children, when the schoolmaster requested someone's presence. A few of the staff members smiled at Dolly. At this Helen coughed, the smug maids became silent as they tensed in embarrassment.

As Helen expected, Dolly's expression had made the early morning bags under Dolly's eyes all but disappear.

With her eyes darting from right to left, Dolly looked surprised at Helen's request. She exited her seat and followed Helen to the office, not helped because Helen didn't make a habit of having these disciplinary conversations early in the morning. She felt it disrupted too much of the smooth workings of the house. Still, Helen wanted to get the case going. She must look for leads straight away, so she didn't have time to wait until the evening briefing, to talk to Dolly about the lack of proper dusting on the main staircase. The earlier Helen could get started on the case, the better. Plus, Dolly was new to the job, and Helen didn't want her to develop bad habits.

They both made their way towards Mr Benton's private office, Helen leading the way and Dolly close behind her. Helen could hear Dolly's scuttling gait, trying not to let it get to her as Helen hated it when people didn't pick their feet up.

After both Dolly and Helen had entered the office, Helen instructed Dolly to close the door behind her while Helen made her way to the desk. She waited until Dolly had closed the door behind her, this was when Dolly's breathing became abnormal, her chest rising and falling rapidly. Helen could see Dolly's breathing become more erratic as she grasped at straws as to why Helen needed to talk to her.

'Miss Squireton, I don't know what I've done wrong, but whatever it was I'm terribly sorry, it won't happen again. Please, miss, don't fire me.' The words came out of Dolly's mouth so fast and in such a high-pitched tone that Helen wondered whether Dolly had taken a breath in the time between getting up from the table and entering the office. Realising that Dolly was still talking and offering things she may have done to cause being taken aside, Helen lifted her hand up straight with an outstretched arm.

Helen stood behind her desk in the office that she shared with Mr Benton, containing bookshelves piled high with ledgers of staff records and lists of chores. Some of which went as far back as to when Helen was first enrolled here and some further back still. They made the office smell of worn-out furniture and old crisp paper. As Helen watched, Dolly slowly breathed normally again. Dolly's back straightened, and her chest movement became more regular.

Helen couldn't help but notice, that unlike herself at that age, Dolly was new to life in domestic service in such a large house. Helen had come straight to service for the Ellentons once she became of age, having transferred from families with smaller homes and was more of a mother's help. Dolly had come from a farming background.

Rather than being a seamstress like her mother, Helen opted for domestic service. She couldn't quite remember why, maybe the reason was that Helen had no children, nor was she engaged, so domestic service seemed an obvious choice. She had no one pulling her away from the job she loved. In a way, the Ellentons were her family.

Helen took a moment to read Dolly's demeanour, she stood a little slouched. Maybe because she knew Helen wasn't about to praise her, Helen tried not to become annoyed at Dolly's lack of proper posture.

'I came in the other night after talking to Mr and Mrs Ellenton to find that the ornaments on the stairs had not been dusted properly.' Helen explained, as she took in Dolly, carefully analysing as best she could what Dolly's reaction to this would be. She was clearly in a state of shock with how Helen had called her to accompany her to the office. Helen wondered if she should have waited till later in the day to address this with Dolly, she hadn't realised that having this conversation would distress Dolly this much. Helen didn't want to cause Dolly to get distracted from her duties, but there was no changing it now.

Looking down at her hands, Dolly twisted her fingers around each other. For a moment, she seemed too young to be in domestic service. Passing a moment to deliberate what to do next, Helen then continued.

'The amount of dust suggests you've been neglecting to do your chores properly for some time. I do not tolerate tardiness, Dolly, this cannot go on.' Helen allowed Dolly to digest that there was no need to panic just yet. 'Otherwise, I will have to notify Mr Ellenton that you are no longer suitable for your role, or at the very least need supervision to do your job properly. Neither of which looks good, are we clear?' Helen stated with authority. Helen took a long but measured breath as a small pang of guilt built. She was disciplining Dolly not firing her, neither was she Dolly's mother. Helen didn't have the time, nor the responsibility, for how Dolly responded to teaching, she told herself when the conversation came to a natural pause. However, that didn't stop Helen from feeling uneasy at what she was seeing in front of her, for Dolly was still young.

Dolly shook her head in embarrassment as she repeatedly apologised. With her eyes wide, it wasn't only her voice showing Dolly's sense of how much trouble she could be in. Should Helen notify Mr Ellenton, seeing the panic in Dolly's face, Helen finished the conversation by warning Dolly. After Helen had done so, Dolly continued to wait. An awkward moment passed, each not sure what the other person expected to happen next. Helen realised what Dolly had been standing around for. 'You can get on with your chores now, Dolly,' Helen stated, hoping that she sounded warmer than Detective Arthur the other night, but that wasn't hard to do, Dolly backed away to exit the office, reversing into the door handle.

After Dolly had successfully exited Mr Benton's and Helen's office, Helen set about collecting the freshly ironed newspaper and made her way upstairs with the rest of the service staff, putting together how she would ask for a couple of hours' leave. They knew she may need time off to help the police with the investigation. As far as they understood it, while Helen knew she was the only one doing the investigating, thoughts of the evidence she had compiled lying on her desk filled her head, getting lost in her thoughts. Mr Benton coughed to move Helen on, as the sizeable interior doors opened to a brightly lit room, the morning sun filled the room with its natural light.

Mrs Ellenton had done an excellent job picking colour schemes and soft furnishings that made the most of the wall to ceiling windows. Shades of pinks and white wallpaper, with floral-patterned curtains. Helen blinked a few times, as her eyes adjusted to the sudden influx of light. The fluid movement of the staff serving the Ellentons kept to the perimeter to the room, unless needing to interact with the family. Painting a level of invisibility while they did so, taking their places and accomplished their tasks, it made Helen feel the divide between the two groups of people in the room. She was about to break the glass screen between the staff and the family.

Breathing slowly and shaking her hands by her sides, Helen took a moment to build up the willingness to ask Mr Ellenton if it were possible to go to the police station. She didn't want her staff to consider her actions hypocritical.

Given the conversation she just had with Dolly, it felt almost hypocritical to ask to leave and do something else. Helen reminded herself that Grace needed her to keep working the case and fight for her justice, as she couldn't do herself. She knew she needed to ask permission, but Helen had just had a day off, what would Helen do if he said no? Helen could do it in her break, but that would mean a less than thorough job, and Helen hated things not being done thoroughly. She had to ask him, there was no avoiding it. Swallowing her anxiety as she flexed her fingers, Helen made ready to burst the divide between her and Mr Ellenton.

Mid breakfast service, Helen handed Mr Benton the paper. With more than Mr Benton now clocking her uncharacteristic behaviour, Helen walked forwards to just in front of the serving staff, head held up and shoulders back. She caught Mr Ellenton's eye, as she coughed softly.

Helen could feel her heartbeat rising as thoughts of how audacious this could seem, made her chest tighten, even though Helen had been in their employ since she was Dolly's age. And at the start of their marriage. Helen took a deep breath and spoke.

Chapter 9

'Excuse me, sorry to bother you at breakfast, sir.' Helen was relieved Dolly wasn't on breakfast service today. That would have made Helen's embarrassment at the spectacle she had become even worse. Helen fought the need to look down. This wasn't the time for shy, submissive behaviour.

'I was wondering if I could attend the police station this morning.' Helen paused, allowing Mr Ellenton to take a bite of his toast before he needed to reply to her request. 'All the servants are aware of what I expect of them today,' Helen asked, feeling her blood warm up. The hairs at the back of her neck stood up straight as all the staff seemed to stop in shock and stare at Helen. She was aware of how out of character her behaviour was. Helen fought the compulsion to twist her fingers around themselves.

Helen noticed a few staff members stared at her and began hushed conversation between themselves. She glanced at one of them, catching the young gentleman by surprise. The staff member stopped the conversation and focused on his duties. Helen may never outrank Mr Ellenton, not only because she was his staff, but she was also a woman, however, she was still higher than the young gentleman serving coffee.

'Yes, Helen, I'm sure Mr Benton can keep an eye out for the servants while you're gone,' Mr Ellenton agreed, slightly blurry-eyed, as he took another bite of breakfast and continued to read the paper.

'Thank you, sir,' Helen said, as the hairs on the back of her neck relaxed. Her blood cooled, grateful for Mr Ellenton's response as she did the same thing that Dolly had done to her before. She stood straight and exited the room, breathing and hoping that she hadn't blushed.

Walking out of the room to grab her belongings before heading out, she put together an argument for Detective Arthur, knowing full well he would not be best pleased to hear that she'd been sleuthing.

Helen did quick work of descending the stairs leading from her bedroom to the kitchen. She had to slalom through the mass of staff packing away the utensils from breakfast and beginning to prepare for the guests to arrive, heads down and conversation minimal. There was relief for an escape and that she'd hadn't offloaded too much on Mr Benton. There shared responsibility of the staff had been forged on a mutual understanding that if they kept to their roles, then everything would run as it should.

Exiting the building via the delivery entrance to the kitchen, Helen made a note that she would need to be ready for an onslaught that Detective Arthur may have prepared for her.

She entered the police station to find Detective Arthur in his office, along with Deputy James, leaning back in the corner, an official-looking case file open in his hands. Helen could tell they were discussing something. She guessed the almost empty-looking folder was her case. Suspecting that they may have finally listened to her, Helen wondered whether they'd picked up the case because Deputy James had pushed for an equivocal death investigation or whether it was Detective Arthur not wanting to be shown up by a woman.

Helen walked in proudly, with head held high and

shoulders back; she was going to make them listen to her even if they didn't want to. She was not going to let Detective Arthur take this away from her, it was her case, not his.

She stood between Deputy James and Detective Arthur's desk, taking in the Detectives' gaze, he was almost red with frustration and anger. She waited for a response from him.

'Miss Squireton, what are you doing here? I told you we will contact you when we have something on the case,' Detective Arthur stated his tone as cold as the stone walls of the station.

'I have suspicions about our case, and by the scene we have here, it looks to me as if you have something about the case, which as you've previously stated, you should have notified me,' Helen argued back as she found a seat opposite Detective Arthur. This time, she would not allow Deputy James to cover for her as if she was unable to stand up for herself. 'The victim I believe, is a young woman by the name of Grace Andrews, she worked at Hexham's solicitors.'

Detective Arthur sighed and stood up. 'Grace Andrews does indeed work at Hexham's solicitors, Mr Hexham told me you had popped in before us, and kindly gave us Grace's belongings from her desk. They are filed, ready for us to look at for evidence once we have a strong lead.' A smug but tired tone only added to Helen's sense that they had only done this to stonewall her. 'I'm disappointed in you, Miss Squireton, you were told not to interfere with the case and yet you to go gallivanting off on your own, without police supervision and potentially put yourself in danger,' he said with a sharp, irritated tone. Helen could see his vain attempts to quell his anger. Helen couldn't help but feel a sense of smugness came over her, it's not pleasant to have your actions be in vain. She continued to justify her reason for being at the station.

'You and I both know you wouldn't have even entertained the idea of investigating the case if I hadn't gone gallivanting off. I was in a place of good public repute, I didn't want to bring down a business while I was simply information gathering,' Helen argued back, causing Detective Arthur to stiffen his jaw as his face turned red, with his fists planted firmly on his desk.

'This is now a murder investigation, Miss Squireton, and you must now leave it to us, the police, to investigate it in peace.' He indicated for her to leave. 'I will send someone to you if we need information from you.'

Helen couldn't help her face making all sorts of unbecoming looks as she descended the stairs from the station to the street. All she had done was identify the victim as Grace Andrews and her probable whereabouts before she had died in Helen's arms. It was most certainly not enough information to have warranted any attention from the perpetrator. Feeling a little defeated, Helen made her way home.

'Miss Squireton,' Deputy James called after her. Helen stopped to allow him to catch up, as he was tall, it did not take long.

'Deputy James,' Helen greeted him once he caught up with her, a little puzzled as to why he had chased after her, hoping he wasn't about to try and excuse his boss's behaviour towards her.

'I don't agree with the way Detective Arthur treated you, I saw the young woman die too, and I can't help but agree with you that it seemed odd that she died so violently and so suddenly. I also want to pursue the case, and if there is an offender to be found, I want to find him. Detective Arthur doesn't seem to be convinced.' Benjamin paused gauging Helen's reaction.

'I got that impression from him also, Benjamin. Is there anything else? I have things to do,' Helen replied still feeling a little hurt over her conversation with Detective Arthur.

'So, I'm going to tell you what we were discussing before you came into the station, but you mustn't let on that it was me who told you, are we clear?' Deputy James indicated with a sense of urgency, not wanting to be gone from Detective Arthur for too long, given he was still on his shift. His time out of the station was limited, as he eagerly waited for a response from Helen. Helen was relieved that he hadn't gone out of his way to defend Detective Arthur or justify his actions.

'Yes, Deputy James, if it comes up, I won't tell the Detective I got the information from you, what was it you were talking about?' Helen asked, breathing slowly to calm herself so she could listen to what Deputy James was about to say.

'We were talking about the pathologist's report when you entered, it mentions that there are signs of poison having been used, then as she may have been drinking, we think that might be the cause of death. We don't know the symptoms well enough, as I was only there once the poison started to kill Grace. I'm going to push Detective Arthur to pursue the case as if it's a murder case, if not I'll take on the case myself. But do me a favour, let me handle Detective Arthur from here on in. If you pursue this case as a civilian, it won't make it to court, and any evidence you may have gathered may be null and void due to it not being gathered following procedure. I'm sure you understand,' Deputy James said with a smile.

'I see, yes, Deputy James, I understand,' Helen replied, puzzled as to why Deputy James had told her this if she was not allowed to get involved in the murder case.

'Are you free tomorrow evening at about seven o'clock?' Deputy James asked.

Thinking for a moment, Helen replied, 'Yes, Benjamin, I am.' Trying to suppress the feeling of excitement.

'I would like to take you for a drink tomorrow. I would like to know you better,' Deputy James asked, not doing a great job at suppressing his excitement, as a smile slowly spread across his face.

'That would be lovely, Benjamin, thank you,' Helen replied with a hint of laughter at the young man in front of her.

'My shift ends at six, so I'll pick you up at seven,' Deputy James replied, making his way back to the station.

Chapter 10

Waiting for Deputy James to arrive, Helen found herself feeling at a loss in her navy blue with white trim casual dress and small kitten heels. Fixing her skirt and pulling at her sleeves Helen remembered the dread at the thought that it'd been so long since she wore it, it may not fit her anymore.

With spending so much time in the same uniform day in day out, Helen felt strange wearing anything else. Lifting her hand, Helen checked on the casual hairdo she had put her hair in.

She remembered scurrying down her stairs and into the kitchen on her way to the staff entrance, watching as Dolly muttered and stared at their boss dressed unusually. Make-up on and in heels, Helen realised that they may have never seen her in anything else other than in her uniform. It must have been as strange for them seeing her in her casual outfit as Helen felt wearing it.

Helen was thankful for the trip she had taken into town with her mother while she'd been ill. They had taken a walk along the beach one summer, and on the way back to the family home, her mother had spotted the dress in a shop window.

'Helen, you'd look good in that, why don't we go in, and you can try it on,' she'd suggested. Helen had joked her mother was up to something but thought better of denying her sick mother the joy of dress shopping. As she stood to wait for

Benjamin, Helen was thankful that her mother had made her get it.

Getting impatient with excitement, Helen made one last check to make sure she was presentable before standing on her tiptoes to see Benjamin's cab pull up to her as Benjamin smiled out the window at her. 'Benjamin,' Helen called out a little over-enthusiastically. The following embarrassment at how that had sounded, temporarily engulfed her, but quickly changed to a slightly calmer form of butterflies.

'Helen,' Benjamin greeted her when she had sat down. He sounded just as eager and excitable as Helen felt.

'Where are we off to then?' Helen asked chirpily, as she tried to calm the butterflies in her stomach. Her heart was racing in her chest so fast that she could hear it in her ears. Helen placed her hands on her lap, looking out of the window, to try to keep some sort of decorum.

'I've been told the Locus Nectar is the place to go.' Benjamin paused, trying to read Helen's expression. Helen hoped he would fail for she felt like a small schoolchild on her first day of school, before the realisation of leaving their parents kicked in. 'Unless you've anywhere else you'd rather go?'

Helen thought there would be a chance that Henry, upon seeing Helen with Deputy James, could cause a scene, taking what was just a simple drink as being spied on. However, being at the Locus Nectar could put Helen in a position to find out who was grieving for Grace and who was unremorseful.

Helen knew that the punters in pubs weren't too much different to the ladies that Mrs Ellenton entertained for afternoon tea or bridge, there was bound to be the odd punter talking about the lack of Grace's presence. They'll be another one talking about how she was there in spirit and in their thoughts, allowing Helen to look for who was mourning Grace's death and who wasn't.

'The Locus Nectar is perfect, Benjamin,' Helen answered, excitement returning to her stomach. Another wave of butterflies hit Helen, as a bump in the road nearly sent Helen into the roof of the cab. Benjamin looked her way, a little worried that she may fall off her seat. Seeing Helen keeping herself in her place, he relaxed and leant back in his own.

Looking around the bar as they entered the Locus Nectar for somewhere they could sit and enjoy their drinks, Helen couldn't help but wonder the reason for the bar to be unusually quiet given the time of day it was. She wondered if it was a reaction from the punters to Grace's death.

'That looks like a good spot, Benjamin, we'll sit over there,' Helen suggested, pointing towards a booth in the corner of the room.

Benjamin looked at where she was pointing then replied, 'Yes, let's do that.'

Making their way to the bar, Helen could feel her heartbeat rise as the realisation that this was the first conversation Henry and herself had since she was here asking about Grace, now she was here with Benjamin. He was the police, if Henry knew something or indeed had a hand in Grace's death this would not look good to him. Benjamin greeted Henry. Helen saw Henry's expression change from one of bemusement to that of a calm professional. Benjamin asked if they could have their drinks taken to them as it was quiet. Henry nodded.

'What would you like?' asked Henry as he cleared away something underneath the bar. Helen couldn't help but wonder what it was that Henry wanted to hide from either her or from Benjamin. She was just a head of house looking to fill a vacancy and Benjamin. However, a police officer, was off duty.

Helen looked at the choices of these new cocktails that were emerging, while Benjamin was straight in with half a pint of beer.

'What would you like, Helen?' Benjamin asked with a light, gentle tone.

'A small glass of red would be good please,' Helen replied, sounding almost automatic.

After he'd finished paying for the drinks, Benjamin smiled at her as he stepped aside to let her make her way to the booth she'd spotted near the window at the far side of the bar. Benjamin waited for Helen to settle in her seat, which took time as it was a tight squeeze, even for Helen, before taking his own. He leant back and began to drum a tune on the table with his fingers, looking out of the window. Helen could see a few punters start to make their way up the street from the lace mills.

Henry came with their drinks. Helen found her muscles tensing so much they hurt and gripped on to the underside of the table until after their drinks had arrived. The conversation started.

'So, Helen, tell me about your family, you must have some family somewhere,' Benjamin joked.

Helen answered, 'My father is a doctor, he has a surgery in town not far from here.' Then she paused as she played with her wine glass for a moment, watching the red liquid swirl in the glass.

'Is this where you got your ability to check for injuries?' Benjamin added.

'Probably,' Helen answered with a sheepish smile. 'My mother is a seamstress, and she works at home as it meant, in the early days, that she could be at home looking after my two brothers and me. My oldest brother, Edward, was lost to the Great War, and my youngest is still kicking about, he's my father's apprentice. How about you?' Helen asked back.

'I'm an orphan, I'm told I was unexpected, and my parents didn't have the means to care for me,' Benjamin began, pausing to take a sip from his drink. 'In my early teens, I got into numerous fights on the street with the other street boys. That's when I met Detective Arthur, and he offered me a chance to be an apprentice, if I wished to after the apprenticeship was over, I could stay on. I've never looked back since,' Benjamin answered with a mix of remorse and chirpiness.

Helen took a sip of her drink and shifted a little before asking about Detective Arthur. A part of her wondered whether it would be impertinent to ask, but she needed to make some sense as to why Detective Arthur, as she knew him, would take on a street kid. The two-character traits didn't seem to match up.

'Has he always been that sharp towards people, Benjamin, or is it just me?'

Benjamin swirled his beer a little, he was thinking deeply about what his answer would be. There was no doubt Detective Arthur had a chequered past.

Benjamin began shaking his head. 'No, he was more agreeable to people.' Benjamin took a breath. Helen wondered if she'd hit a nerve. 'Until he lost his wife and daughter to Spanish flu. Detective Arthur never got over it, his daughter's room is the same as she left it, he still organises his clothes the way his wife used to.'

Benjamin took another gulp of his beer as Helen reflected on what she had heard.

Just as Helen was draining her drink, she noticed the receptionist from the solicitor's rush in from the street and go directly to Henry. Nothing about this interaction was notably unusual – she could really need a drink. Helen thought there was something in the way she clung to Henry. Somewhat like a child seeking protection from an adult figure.

The receptionist Helen saw at Mr Hexham's was upright and professional, but the woman she saw here was fearful and coward-like. She was clinging on to him as she talked in fear of something or someone.

Helen watched as the scene unfurled. Henry was not himself either, forcefully moving his arm from the woman's grasp and giving her a hard stare, he muttered something that gave Helen the chills.

Watching Helen as she shivered and raised her hand to her arms, Benjamin asked, 'Are you cold, Helen?' He began taking his jacket off to give it to her.

'No, I'm fine, I'm wondering if it could be possible to either talk to your pathologist or read the pathology report?' Helen asked, keeping an eye on the young woman. As she'd been forced to leave, she wiped away a tear, sniffling. Helen watched as the receptionist tried to regain some composure. Helen realised that she had a sense of weariness about her she had not seen before, her lip quivering as she marched out of the bar.

Sitting back for a moment, pondering Helen's request, giving nothing away as he did so, Benjamin finally spoke. 'The pathology report can't leave the station, and technically you shouldn't be able to read it. But as the case is now a murder case, I can bring you in under the cover that you are a consultant and let you read it with myself always present,' Benjamin replied with a smile as he settled back down in his seat.

Helen laughed. 'All right, Benjamin, I suppose that's fair.' Benjamin's face turned serious.

'Remember, Helen, you're my consultant, everything you do needs to either come straight back to me or needs to be done with me present, is that clear?'

'Yes, Benjamin, perfectly clear,' Helen replied, taking a small sip of her drink.

There was a break in their conversation. Helen heard Henry speaking to someone on the phone. The noise was so loud that Helen had to strain her ears to listen to exactly what Henry was saying. Still, she did notice him saying something about taking a rain check, a phrase not commonly used in English but rather an American colloquialism for postponing something. Helen decided it was time to end the evening.

'We both have work to do tomorrow, Deputy James,' she announced as she gathered their glasses, placing them on a tray and moved the dish close to the end of the table.

'Indeed, we do, Miss Squireton. Indeed, we do,' Benjamin replied as he slid out of the booth and nodded to Henry as they left.

Benjamin let Helen pass him as he lifted his jacket over his shoulders then he quickened his step to open the door for her. Pulling her cardigan closer around her, she took his arm. They set off negotiating the ever-growing crowds, aiming for the main street.

Once they had reached the main street, both climbed into a cab. Again, Benjamin helped Helen take her seat before grabbing his own and ordering the driver to take them to the Ellentons' first then back to his address.

Helen began to look out of the window, watching the scenery change between dirty built-up streets to the fresh air of the slightly statelier homes. She thought about Henry's use of American terminology as he spoke, he never did it when Henry talked to people if he did, he was quick to translate. Was Henry actually American? Helen noted that the bar did seem to appear and become popular quickly. Henry seemed to have come out of nowhere when the bar opened. Helen remembered the newspaper covering it, there was no mention of any family when the reporter wrote the article. Just then, Helen noticed Benjamin staring at her.

'You shouldn't stare, Benjamin,' Helen firmly but playfully mentioned.

Benjamin smiled and sheepishly looked down at his hands as he smiled, revealing his white teeth, again. 'Sorry, you look stunning, Helen.'

Helen was not sure how to respond to this observation, for she wasn't used to this type of attention if any, as work required her to fade into the background, become a ghost in the Ellentons' house.

'Thank you, Benjamin, it's been a long time since I've been in something other than my uniform,' Helen replied, a little unsettled at her outfit again, worried about how Benjamin was seeing her. Helen continued to look out of the cab window.

Jumping out of the cab to help Helen out, Benjamin held Helen's hand a little tighter than one would expect. Helen suppressed a smile, not wanting to let Benjamin know that she had noticed him holding her hand a little faster.

Benjamin went to jump back into the cab, then hesitated,

not wanting to leave Helen to go into the house without a proper goodbye. He realised he still had Helen's hand.

'Can we do this again sometime?' he asked almost scared that Helen may brush him off.

'Yes, Benjamin, I look forward to it,' Helen whispered.

Watching as the cab begin to pull away, Helen felt a wave of childish excitement, she had been so focused on working for the Ellentons that she often missed opportunities to go out socially, as her job required for her to spend most evenings working.

Chapter 11

Unpinning her hair for bed and placing her pins in a dish, Helen reminisced on the evening she had spent with Deputy James, how he was ever so eager to make sure she had a pleasant evening, offering his jacket to keep her warm. She wasn't shivering because of the cold, but because of the interaction between the receptionist and Henry.

As usual, her mind was never fully distracted from the case. Helen's thoughts drifted back to two questions that had not left her mind since she'd been in the Locus Nectar with Benjamin. Question one. What made the receptionist so fearful, was it Henry that made her afraid, had she gone to make amends or to seek protection? Question two. Helen needed to find out Henry's personal history, where had he come from before running the Locus Nectar?

Setting about going to bed, she'd wondered about what had been said a few days earlier, mentioning that they were looking for the cause of death being poison. After pausing in her thoughts for a moment, she wondered what poison would do such a thing the way it did. After searching her mind for options with no success, she decided it was time to sleep. She'd be no good to anyone half dead herself with exhaustion.

Waking a little earlier than usual, Helen collected her thoughts on the case. She knew the victim to be Grace Andrews, and that she was employed at Mr Hexham's solicitors. Helen noted Grace's colleague in the office opposite Mr Hexham's. The way she scolded Helen, left her to wonder, did she know something about Grace's death? Then there's Mr Hexham's adverse reaction to Helen's questions, about the death of one of his employees, wasn't exactly professional. The way he bounced around from one feeling to another, Helen reflected on what may have caused such a response from either of them.

Breathing and muttering something to herself that she didn't quite understand, she picked up her pen. She needed to remember this.

Helen scribbled away at her desk, noting that Grace may have frequented the Locus Nectar on the night someone murdered her.

The latest information was, the police now believed she was right – it was a murder, prompting them, well Deputy James, to launch a murder investigation. There was evidence that Grace was poisoned. Leaving the question, which poison? Helen thought back to what she saw when Grace fell into her arms.

Helen remembered the way that Grace was clawing at her neck in such a way as if she was choking, showing that she was having difficulty breathing but nothing threatening around her neck. Then the convulsions. One would assume a fit, however, if you were prone to those, would you not be best to stay away from alcohol? Then there were the signs of risus sardonicus, which Helen knew was the pulling of the facial muscles manifesting in a grim-like expression which showed on the victim's face. What could have such an effect on someone's body?

Sitting back in her chair and glancing at her watch, it

would be time to get started soon, but she knew how she could still get answers. While out doing errands, she could check-in at the police station to share her theory about Henry being American and see if Benjamin could trace any of Henry's personal history.

Chapter 12

After supervising the organising of a large delivery of household goods, Helen popped her head around the door of Mr Benton's office and excused herself for a while.

'I'm just off into town to check on a few errands, I'll be back in about an hour,' she said as Mr Benton had his head down, busying himself with balancing the books ready for Mr Ellenton to look over when he had the time in an evening. Hearing her request to leave, he nodded and waved her off without a break in his concentration.

She could hear her heels clicking as she turned the corner that led out away from the house, feeling the air changing from an early morning chill to the warmth of the mid-morning sun, however fleeting it would be. Helen made sure her cardigan was around her. She made her way into town.

She wondered how she would get the information on what poison killed Grace. She had a list of people she believed could have given the poison to Grace. So that was the piece of the puzzle of who committed the crime on its way to being solved. At least she had narrowed it down to a handful of people, albeit based on nothing but the way they reacted either to the news or her presence at a particular place at a specific time.

Helen needed to find how the pieces of the puzzle fitted together, poisons were hard things to figure out, she knew there were lots of things to getting it right, the weight of a person, a smaller person, meant a lower dose. Then there would be what poison. There were a few you could choose from, some over the counter and some harder to get hold of. Some kill faster than others, leaving you less time to create an alibi.

Helen's mind spun so much with her thoughts. Helen almost missed the station house, halting to cross the road, apologising to an elderly woman who nearly collided with her. None of her suspects, Helen thought, had that kind of knowledge.

Entering the station, Helen began looking for Deputy James but found Detective Arthur standing in the lobby, with a face of thunder roll over him as Helen made her way towards him.

'I'm looking for Deputy James, Detective, you wouldn't know of his whereabouts?' Helen asked, but all the while wondering what had gone on between the two gentlemen while she had been away from the station.

'He's in the autopsy room, Miss Squireton, waiting for you,' he answered, still not taking his eyes away from her. Helen nodded and made her way back out of the station and back in the side entrance leading to where both Deputy James and herself had logged the body a couple of evenings ago. Helen noticed Detective Arthur had followed her not long after she'd left the building. It seemed to Helen that he was still to be kept appraised of matters even if Deputy James had taken on the case himself.

Knocking on the autopsy room door, Helen could hear Benjamin call for her to enter.

'William, this is Miss Squireton, she is my consultant on the case. Miss Squireton, this is our pathologist, Mr William

Roy.' Helen came to stand next to Benjamin and exchanged greetings with Mr Roy.

'Deputy James mentioned you saw signs of poisoning Mr Roy, I was wondering if I could see the pathology report myself. That way we're all able to draw out similarities between what I saw when I had carried Grace out of the alleyway where I first saw her and what you've found in your report.'

Mr Roy looked towards Benjamin for a moment, he was asking whether it was okay to do this. Benjamin nodded, and Mr Roy obliged, handing over the pathology report. Mr Roy asked, 'How did the victim seem when you saw her? I ask because depending on the poison, people react differently, some poison induces panic, some make their victim go as high as a kite, and then they die.'

Just as Helen was about to answer, having only just picked up the report, Detective Arthur burst in. Seeing that Helen had the pathology report in her hands he stepped closer, making to take it off her. In perfect synchronicity, Benjamin stepped forward as Helen turned away from the Detective.

'Miss Squireton is my consultant and my only witness in my case, Detective, you're here to assist me only,' Benjamin spoke firmly as he stepped away, keeping a close eye on his superior for now.

'She looked frightened, Mr Roy, agitated, she couldn't walk properly as her legs had become rigid. She had started to convulse while we were in the alleyway, there was some shortness of breath, but that could be part of the convulsions, could it not, Mr Roy?' Helen asked. Mr Roy nodded, a sombre look on his face.

'Do we know what poison was used, Mr Roy?' Benjamin

asked, a twinge of either eagerness or excitement in his voice. Then Benjamin shuffled slightly, not wanting to look insensitive over the fact that this woman had died.

'Yes, Deputy James, there is one more thing I'd like to check, but I believe we do,' Mr Roy answered, his voice matching his expression.

'What do you think killed her, Mr Roy?' Deputy James asked.

'Strychnine, sir,' Mr Roy stated. 'It's a particularly nasty way to die, there is one last thing I'd like to check first, but it's looking probable that she was poisoned with that particular drug.'

'Is there anything we need to know about this drug, Mr Roy?' Benjamin asked, turning slightly towards the door.

'Yes, sir, only three milligrams of this poison are lethal to humankind as well as other animals,' Mr Roy stated. 'Symptoms of this poison show after only fifteen to twenty minutes after exposure.' He paused for a moment and continued to describe everything that Helen had seen. 'I'd like to take a urine sample to solidify what I have found, but as I said, it's looking likely that strychnine was used in the woman's death.'

'Thank you, Mr Roy,' Benjamin replied, turning towards the door.

'I need to speak to you, Deputy James,' Helen called to him as he strode off back to the station. Benjamin paused momentarily to let Helen catch up.

'We'll talk in my office. Detective, would you like to join us?' Benjamin called out. Detective Arthur mumbled something under his breath but made efforts to catch up with them all the same.

Once in his office, Helen and Benjamin took a seat and the Detective stood in a corner by the window. 'What do you need to tell me, Miss Squireton?' Benjamin asked. He spoke, Helen knew that Benjamin knew it was something good, or at least helpful.

'I believe Henry, the bartender from the Locus Nectar to be American. There's not much about him that I can find at least, past the article he has on a frame in the back of the bar about him opening the Locus Nectar. His vocabulary is odd, I keep hearing him use American colloquialisms for things such as rain check and trash, rather than rubbish, and then correcting himself.' Benjamin nodded as Detective Arthur sighed in disbelief.

'You need more than that for someone to be a suspect, Miss Squireton,' Detective Arthur retorted, shifting in his corner, agitated at her presence. Turning towards Deputy James, he argued, 'I told you, bringing her into the investigation was a bad idea.'

'That's true, Detective, but it's a start. Carry on, Miss Squireton,' Deputy James prompted.

'There is also the fact that he brews his own beer at times when the stock is low. This means he has access to chemicals, has a high level of skill when it comes to chemistry and would know how to administer poison if Grace was indeed at the Locus Nectar. He'd be able to spike her drink. I remember Grace being at the bar a few times with a cocktail in her hand.'

Both men pondered on this for a moment, then Detective Arthur piped up again. 'Strychnine is also found in pills used to treat certain illnesses. Yes, it could be in her system, but it could be that she has a medical condition we don't know about, there may not be a sinister solution to this case after all.'

'We can find that out, Detective. You do have a point, but if Grace works for a solicitor, she would be smart enough not to drink so close to taking medication, surely.' Deputy James offered this, trying to keep the peace between the three of them. 'How about, you investigate Grace's medical history, and Miss Squireton and I go to the Locus Nectar this evening and ask whether or not Grace had a tipple of choice. That way we can chase two theories at once.' This barely pleased Detective Arthur. Helen was just glad to be taken seriously. Detective Arthur left the office, still a little put out that Helen was involved in the case, leaving Helen and Deputy James alone for a moment.

'I don't think it'll be wise to approach Henry about him being American just yet, Helen, if he is the man we are looking for, then we need evidence to put to him first. But at least we have a suspect now,' Benjamin spoke at a whisper. Helen wondered why he did this as it was just the two of them in the room, but she nodded and returned home for the evening.

The next day, Helen could barely pay attention to her tasks, the lead she had was all that occupied her mind. She needed to find time to tell Deputy James about Mr Hexham's reaction to the news of Grace's death, indicating that there is more of a connection there than him merely being her employer. Finally, the time came when there was a gap in the timing of the chores where Helen could go to the station, while other staff members made coffee or set about organising the equipment they'd used.

Sighing with relief, Helen excused herself. Once again, she made for the station, arriving to find both Deputy James and Detective Arthur in the Deputy James's office.

'You can't keep your nose out can you, Miss Squireton,'

Detective Arthur retorted.

'I have further information that I believe you need to hear, Detective Arthur. I wouldn't want to omit information when it may well help solve the case,' Helen replied, dangling the information like a carrot. Helen couldn't help but let the fact that she knew they needed the information she had fuel her confidence.

'What have you got, Miss Squireton,' Deputy James sat in his chair a smug smile on his face. Helen began to wonder whether he was enjoying her defiance a little too much.

'I know of another potential suspect, who at the time of me speaking to him had rat poison in his immediate vicinity,' Helen explained.

Detective Arthur had heard enough and said, raising his voice just enough to fill his office but not so the whole station could listen to. 'You've been questioning suspects without a police officer present. Deputy James, you need to close her out of the case now before she invalidates any evidence obtained.' Breathing in once again and closing his eyes, his chest shook with the effort of controlling his temper.

'Who is this suspect, Miss Squireton?' Deputy James asked, giving a stern look to Detective Arthur who slumped back into his corner of the room as Deputy James slid his chair out from under the desk slightly.

'Mr Hexham, Deputy, he is Grace's employer. While I was having a conversation with him to inform him of Grace's death, the reaction from him after I had told him that Grace had died was far too extreme for him to be just an employer. I think that there is more to his connection to Grace than meets the eye.' Helen waited for a moment longer. Then the Detective spoke again.

'The silly girl probably drank too much and was on

medication, thus killing herself,' Detective Arthur retorted. At this, Deputy James rolled his eyes. Helen stood there, shocked for a moment, to see Detective Arthur have so little regard for the young woman's life. A girl who must have been his daughter's age had she been alive at the time. Not blinking was the only thing she could do to stop herself from crying.

'Grace Andrews, her name was Grace Andrews, Detective. She died in your division, on your watch,' Helen said as her eyes filled up with tears of remorse and anger, at the lack of response. Helen turned and made her way home to finish up at the Ellentons.'

Chapter 13

The next day, Helen made for the solicitors, determined to prove to Detective Arthur that she and Benjamin were right to pursue this as a murder case. Pushing the large door into Mr Hexham's solicitors, the bell rang, knocking Helen's focus back to reality. Her mind ready to balance tact and diplomacy while getting the information she would need to continue with her investigation. The smell of freshly printed ink filled the air, with the sun beaming down through the windows lighting the room with an early autumn morning warmth.

'Can I help you?' came the voice of the receptionist, less chirpily than the last time Helen was here. Helen wondered why the young receptionist felt the need to be sharp with her, she had done nothing, at least that she was aware of, to offend her. Helen decided it was best not to give away anything to the young receptionist until she had a better understanding of what had happened to Grace.

'I have come to see Mr Hexham,' Helen replied.

'I'll let him know you're here,' the receptionist said not ready to take her eyes off Helen. There was a chill in the air, the receptionist drifted slowly towards wherever Mr Hexham was, but returning a little while later without Mr Hexham. Helen sat back in her seat and waited for him to see her, all the while, wondering why he hadn't come straight out. The office wasn't busy, neither was he with another client. The only sound in the whole office was the sound of typewriters. Helen's mind turned back to the receptionist.

Helen's eyes widened a little in shock at the tone the young receptionist had taken with her. She had barely spoken to her other than to ask for Mr Hexham. She was no threat to the young receptionist, not now anyway, not unless Helen's theory that the young receptionist and Henry being suspects held truth. Nevertheless, Helen knew she needed to offer some sort of peace offering, looking around as she did so she noticed someone had got round to re-labelling the cabinets that stood aside where Helen sat; an appropriate peace offering came to her.

'I'm sorry about your co-worker; the world seems a little dimmer without her.' Helen attempted to fill the silence sympathetically.

The receptionist looked up from the typewriter replied, sharply, 'It has nothing to do with me, and I wasn't there.'

The receptionist halted, her eyes widening as Helen's head spun as you do when you've heard something of particular interest. The two of them froze intensely in silence.

Helen was about to ask the receptionist what she meant by I wasn't there, for Helen had not accused her of anything yet, when Mr Hexham entered the room, eyes red and puffy. She noticed a black band around his upper arm. Helen noted he was still in mourning attire, not usual behaviour for an employer to be mourning in such a way. This only confirmed her suspicions that Mr Hexham was connected to Grace more deeply than she first thought.

'Miss Squireton, would you like to come through,' Mr Hexham asked with a quiver in his voice.

Turning to face Mr Hexham, Helen broke the

awkwardness as neither the young receptionist nor Helen wanted to look away. She needed to speak to Mr Hexham, that is what she had come for.

'Before you go, sir, I have a personal matter to attend to, could I be excused for a moment?' asked the receptionist. Getting up from her desk to make a move to leave, before Mr Hexham had given her his permission. No one moved for a moment, Helen watched the receptionist, keeping one eye on the door, poised, body tense and stiff, ready to bolt out the door. Her whole body was poised, ready to escape.

Puzzled at this, there was an air about the receptionist of someone who wanted to escape, leading Helen to wonder whether she'd wanted to avoid her. Still, where to Helen thought. Given her recent behaviour, Helen figured it would be to the Locus Nectar and to Henry as she'd done a few times recently. She would run out of the office onto the street and into the Locus Nectar and to Henry.

Helen's mind whirled with speculation so much her head began to throb with pain, she had to remind herself that speculating wouldn't get her anywhere. She needed fact not theory if she were to find out who killed Grace.

'Yes, Mary, you can leave for a moment, but be back by my next appointment, I may need you to make notes,' Mr Hexham stated as they both made their way to his office.

'Have you got anywhere regarding Grace's death; do you know who did this to her?' Mr Hexham asked as he suppressed a tear, his voice quivering a little, as he mentioned Grace's name. Helen watched him for a moment as his head lowered with a painful memory of her.

'Unfortunately, Mr Hexham, I can't tell you. However, I do need to develop bearing on what type of character Grace was, what can you tell me about her?' Helen asked delicately, not wanting to cause any more distress to the elderly man.

Helen understood the feeling of grief that losing an employee can have, even a distant employee. Still, for Mr Hexham to be grieving quite this much was slightly irregular and unprofessional. The grief-stricken man that Helen saw before her matched that of someone losing a loved one, adding to Helen's suspicion about there being more to the connection between him and Grace that met the eye. Helen wondered whether he would get defensive at her again. She knew that grief could cause unpredictable mood swings and Mr Hexham was most definitely grieving and had shown to be variable in his reaction towards Helen. Helen couldn't help herself but puzzle over this in a way you may think hard about placing a puzzle piece in the correct place when it's not apparent.

'Grace was a brilliant young woman; she had a zest for life that I'd never seen before.' Mr Hexham stared into nothingness as he brought her back to his memories. 'She worked hard, and though working for me wasn't her passion, she always took pride in working at whatever task I gave her to do. A voice like an angel, that was my Grace.' Mr Hexham shed a tear while Helen made a mental note.

Something about Mr Hexham referring to Grace in such a way added to Helen's confusion. Looking about the room for a moment, Helen noticed small pellets lying around the room and along the bookshelves.

'Do you have a rodent problem again Mr Hexham?' Helen asked.

Mr Hexham's tone turned cold. 'I think you should leave now, Miss Squireton, I have applications to shortlist.'

Taken aback by Mr Hexham's change in demeanour,

Helen could feel herself being pushed back into her seat with the surprise. She understood that being asked if he had a rodent problem would not go down well, and he was indeed offended, but to go from barely being able to stand to suddenly not only be able to stand but to stand tall, was baffling. His chest widened on the defensive was an extreme change in mood, most certainly hiding something, Helen concluded, but did it relate to Grace, and how?

Helen calmed herself down and explained that it was a question of no consequence and she merely asked out of curiosity in a bid to calm Mr Hexham down, watching as he took a breath.

'It is rat season,' he explained, still defensive towards Helen. 'It's a precautionary measure, I hold important files here.'

Helen excused herself and left. Her mind focused on the new questions she had. What made Grace Mr Hexham's, as far as Helen was aware they weren't father and daughter for her surname was Andrews, not Hexham. Neither did she have a wedding band on her finger, she also didn't behave like a wife would behave, presuming, they had a happy marriage. Still, the grief shown by Mr Hexham surely meant there was more to their relationship. There was one thing Helen was sure on, there was more to Mr Hexham's relationship with Grace than first met the eye, Helen thought as she walked out onto the street to go about her day. She planned how to pass this information on to Deputy James, preferably without Detective Arthur present.

As she passed the Locus Nectar on her way home, Helen noticed the receptionist she now knew was called Mary leaving with a face full of either stern determination or one of suppressed fear. Helen watched as Mary strode off with her back tense and straight. Taking long strides away from the Locus Nectar, her head focused on a single thing. Mary moved as if nothing other than what she'd focused on mattered as she walked with purpose out onto the street, her mind focused on the course of action she would take.

Knowing that Mary had already been in the Locus Nectar earlier that week to talk to Henry and had been shrugged off, Helen couldn't help but think she had tried again to speak to him. This time, she succeeded. Whatever they were up to, whatever it was that Helen had uncovered, they now had a plan, and Helen knew it was not good.

As Helen walked past the large window in the front of the bar, she peered in, wanting to see how Henry had reacted to the plan they had made.

The result was disappointing, where Mary had come out of the bar with a renewed sense of purpose, Henry was unfazed by whatever it was they were about to do. He was stood behind the bar with his usual bubbly smile and a laugh that echoed out onto the nearby street.

That was the second time in as many days, Helen had seen Mary in that bar riled by something. 'The game is afoot.' Helen spoke quietly to herself.

Chapter 14

As Helen made her way through her morning chores, Mr Benton came up to her in the kitchen. 'A letter for you, Miss Squireton.' Looking a little surprised, Helen took it from him. Looking at it, she immediately recognised the handwriting. It was from Benjamin. A tingle of excitement came over her as she flipped it over to open it. Once Helen did, the excitement faded, for she had noticed the police logo on the top of the letter. On it was simply:

Helen, I want to question Henry at lunch. I thought you'd like to come with me, meet me at the top of the street where the bar is, and we'll do this together, just you and me.

Her excitement grew a little. This was the opportunity she'd been looking for to tell Benjamin about Mr Hexham and Mary, her two new suspects, and go through her timeline with him.

Waiting for him at the top of the street, Helen began to put together what she had seen so far. Mr Hexham had rat pellets in his office, and there was the odd reaction Mary had towards Helen when she offered her condolences about her colleague. Was there a love connection between Mr Hexham and Grace? Helen needed to prove it.

'Helen,' came Benjamin's voice he stood next to her, before she realised he had arrived. 'I have some more information about the case you might need to know, do you have time to come back with me to the station after we've questioned Henry?' Benjamin, sounding hopeful.

'Yes, Benjamin, I also have some additional information you need to know about.' Benjamin nodded in reply as they made their way towards the bar. Just before entering, Benjamin stopped and faced Helen.

'Remember, Helen, you're a civilian, not a police officer, I know you have your questions, but for now, please route your questions through me.' Helen sighed then nodded. Benjamin smiled as he stroked her chin. This didn't do much to change her mood, but at least she knew he understood.

'Deputy, Helen, how can I help you? I'm guessing this isn't a social visit,' Henry said looking at Helen with a cold glare.

Benjamin coughed, making Henry look at him instead. 'We just have some questions about a Grace Andrews we heard drinks here frequently, Mr Boston, there's nothing to worry about. Was she here last Friday evening at all?' Benjamin began.

Henry shifted his weight. 'I wasn't here last Friday, I was unwell,' Henry answered, still not too pleased at either of them being sat on the barstools in front of him.

'Am I right in thinking you live upstairs, Mr Boston?' Deputy James asked, with a sterner tone to his voice. Helen kept quiet, she wanted to watch Benjamin questioning Henry. Something about it intrigued her.

At this question, Henry tried to change the subject. 'Would you like a drink, either of you?'

At this, both Benjamin and Helen shook their heads, and shifting to a more professional posture on his seat, Benjamin replied, 'They're just questions, Henry, there's nothing to avoid here unless you guilty of something.'

Henry then answered his question. 'Yes, Deputy, I do live in the flat upstairs, but I don't see that, given that I was upstairs sick, how I would know who was downstairs.' Henry's tone became abrasive. Helen watched as Benjamin took notes. He seemed to have not cared for Henry's tone, there was no reaction from him.

'One last thing, for now, Mr Boston, then we'll let you get on, do you have rat poison on the premises currently?' Henry huffed at this. 'It's just a question Mr Boston, answer it and we'll be on our way.'

'No, I don't, Deputy, not presently.' Was all that Henry said. Deputy James picked up his notebook, and putting it back in his pocket, he dismissed both himself and Helen, thanking Henry for his co-operation.

There was silence between Benjamin and Helen all the way to the station. Once in his office, they both sat on their chairs. 'Helen, Detective Arthur has done some digging. There's nothing to back up your hunch about him being an American other than his vocabulary, we'll still investigate it, but we need more evidence. All the Detective is getting are rumours that he might be, but no one knows for certain. Neither do I believe that Henry is as naïve as to who was in the bar when Grace died. I'll have to go to the factory's and ask around the punters to see if they know anything. We've also found from Mr Hexham Grace's home address, she rents from a landlady, who's got a block of flats near the solicitors,' Benjamin said, looking at her a little too closely.

Landlady. Helen couldn't help but be filled with dread at the thought that all the work she had done so far was a waste of time. That the real, case changing evidence had been in Grace's apartment all along. There's something in Grace's home, and I am going to find it. 'Well, I believe that there may be a love connection between Mr Hexham and Grace. I don't know anything about it, it's just a hunch, but his reactions to me questioning him about her, are extreme, more extreme than what we've seen with Henry just now.' Benjamin nodded.

'I hope you're careful when you go off without me. I don't want anything bad happening to you.' Benjamin's tone was soft and caring. Pausing for a moment, Helen noticed the strange demeanour in Benjamin as he mentioned her being careful. He began to look like a lost boy rather than a grown man.

'Of course, Deputy James, I left it there and left.' Deputy James regained some composure as relief began to show on his face. I also think that Mr Hexham's receptionist should be a suspect, on one of my trips to talk to Mr Hexham I offered my condolences to her. Immediately she became defensive and told me she had nothing to do with it, and she wasn't there. A bit odd, don't you think?'

Benjamin nodded in agreement. 'I agree with you, it does all sound a bit odd,' Benjamin said sitting back in his seat, pondering what Helen had said.

'Why ask about rat poison?' Helen asked.

'Huh.' Benjamin spun back around in his chair to face her; he'd been deep in thought.

'At the bar, when you were questioning Henry, why ask about rat poison?'

Benjamin nodded. 'The last test that William did, was to check Grace's urine for traces of strychnine, and it was positive for signs of the poison, without the victim being able to tell us what happened that's as good as we're going to get,' Benjamin explained.

'Well then, I need to get back to work, what are you going to do next, Deputy James?' Helen asked.

'Detective Arthur and I will chase up the leads regarding the Locus Nectar and Henry. Then we'll look at the other leads surrounding Mr Hexham and Mary. I ask you, Helen, to stay away from potentially dangerous suspects or situations without me being present. Remember, anything you do will come back to me. The public may well have seen you out with me. Working with me on this means if you get into trouble, it will find its way back to me. I may have no choice in what I have to do next, do you understand me?'

'Yes, Deputy, I do,' Helen replied softly. She understood he was trying to keep her safe and happy, not an easy job. With that, she left, planning how she would get into Grace's flat to look for evidence without a set of keys, and on her own. Grace was dead, what could be the danger there?

Chapter 15

The following morning, Helen set about her chores, Grace's flat never being far from her mind. She had read Grace's address in the investigation report. Still, Helen couldn't help but think she needed a ruse, a cover story, should anyone bump into her. Helen planned to go to the house during her lunch break. As it was the middle of the working day, there wouldn't be many people around.

Getting ready to go to Grace's flat, Helen brought an extra scarf with her, just in case she needed to hide her face. Helen knew what she was about to do was risky and if Helen was seen by anybody, she didn't want them knowing it was her.

Making her way towards the house, she noticed a short and stout middle-aged woman walking the same direction. Helen swapped sides of the pavement and followed the lady, not knowing if she was a tenant or the landlady herself. Helen felt compelled to follow her for the remaining journey, always keeping a few feet behind her. The woman walked with purpose, dressed in dark clothes. Helen remembered seeing in the newspaper that they had set Grace's funeral for earlier that day, so guessed, if this was the landlady, she had come from the funeral back to the house.

Realising the landlady was about to enter the large white stone building, Helen ducked behind some iron fencing, taking advantage of the shadows to hide and tying her scarf around her face. So, if the landlady looked her way, she wouldn't notice Helen as she disappeared between the shadows of the buildings with her hat pulled tight on her head. Matched with her scarf covering Helen's face, she hoped it would be difficult for the landlady to recognise her, meaning Helen could watch her from a distance without being noticed.

Watching the landlady bend down to pick something up off the floor, Helen strained her neck, seeing if she could glimpse what it was the landlady had picked up. Still, upon watching something glisten, the landlady stood upright and unlocked the door. Helen realised it was a key.

Hiding in an enclave between to large buildings, peering around the corner to keep her eye on where her target was going, Helen prayed no one had seen her and reported her to the police. She didn't want her reckless actions to find their way to Detective Arthur's or Deputy James's knowledge as she felt her heart rate rise in her chest.

She waited for a moment, her legs tensed ready to make a move out of her hiding spot, on to the street and into the house. Watching the door with an unshakeable focus, this was all about timing.

As Helen made ready to go to the door of the grand house, the proprietor flew out the door again. This time with a basket and a light-coloured shawl. Helen estimated she only had a few minutes until she had to leave, any moment more would mean she was discovered by either another tenant or the landlady, so she hotfooted it to the door.

Picking up the plant pot and removing the key from its hiding place, Helen made sure it matched the circle of cleaner concrete so as not to arouse suspicion.

Taking multiple attempts at making sure it was precisely

on the right spot, when Helen finally accomplished putting the plant pot down. She rolled her eyes at herself. At the same time, at work, her attention to detail was an asset to be proud of, outside of work, it only slowed her down.

In, up to Grace's room to find the evidence and out again. You can do this, Grace needs you to do this, Helen thought as she burst through the door and speedily climbed the stairs. There's one thing her years of domestic service had taught her, was how to ascend and descend stairs quickly and as silently as a spirit. Walking up the corridor at speed, Helen felt as if she had run, headfirst into a wall, as the smell of perfume, the same as Grace had on, only more substantial, hit her nose from the corridor.

Chapter 16

Sliding into Grace's room and closing the door behind her, Helen began her observations about the place. Flimsy furniture, simple pale-coloured curtains hung in a half-drawn, half-open way. The bed was made, the corners had been pulled tight; clearly, Grace knew how to set a room. Still, the room had a sense of temporality about it. Nothing about the place showed to Helen that this was Grace's permanent place of residency. Moving boxes were still lying about, Helen knew that Grace had lived in the area for a while. Everything seemed as though Grace was ready to move at a moment's notice, like Grace had made no plans to stay here for long. But the little luxuries she had allowed herself, there was the odd small piece of soft furnishing placed about the room. Moving towards the vanity table and noticing a matching set of tortoiseshell brush and mirror. Helen opened the drawers. In one of them was a blue crushed velvet box, not large but big enough to pique Helen's interest. Opening it, Helen saw it contained a single string of white pearls. Closing the box slowly, making sure not to disturb too much, Helen noticed what looked like a trousseau. In it there were half-completed embroidered cushions and the cut out of what seemed to Helen like a baby's christening gown. All this laid heavy on Helen's mind, Grace had grander plans, all of which were cut short.

Make-up was placed in a corner on the vanity table. Helen

noted that for a young woman Grace seemed to have lipstick and perfume for every occasion, all varying shades. And on another smaller table nearer the door where Helen stood were some spirits and a cocktail maker. Helen wondered how much Grace drank, or were these bottles ornamental?

Seeing Grace's desk, Helen darted towards it with a feeling of excitement tingling through her fingers as she rummaged through the papers. Grace had rent arrears notices piled high. Helen separated them from the rest, while wondering how long Grace had been in debt to the landlady. Her eyes opened wide as she found some different papers. Helen put down the rent outstanding notices and skim read the rest of the letters one of them read:

Grace, my darling,

I can't stop loving you, you are the reason I come to work in the morning and leave late so I can watch you work and go to wherever it is you spend your evening. How I long for you to whittle them away with me more.

Helen skipped the rest and glanced at the end of the letter, signed:

With love, B.

Reading a couple more, Helen became aware her time here was running out, for the owner would be home soon. Helen couldn't see who this B character was?

Helen fell on one from this 'B.' This one had a different tone. Helen read eagerly, for there was now potentially a new suspect as neither of the old ones really spoke killer to her. Never enough motive to kill Grace in each one of their connections to her.

All right, Grace, have it your way, nothing will change the way I feel for you, but I will love and admire you from a distance.

Hearing a set of heavyset feet make their way down the corridor, getting louder, Helen didn't want to risk the fact that it was another tenant who would just walk on past and not enter Grace's room. Helen ducked behind the door. Calming herself down, you won't be able to talk yourself out of this, if you can't think clearly and then that'll be you, and Grace's justice done for. Helen fought the urge to move and run out the door, letters in hand.

Keeping her eyes on the door, she watched as the shadow behind the door turned to face Grace's room, holding her breath as the doorknob turned and the door creaked.

Helen held her breath as she slowly tucked the letters into her scarf where they would escape anybody's notice as she stood, muscles tense and eyes locked on her one and only exit. If she needed to leave the room, it would have to be through whoever was on the other side of the door.

Watching as the door opened just a little, Helen expected the person to enter, but nothing happened for a moment. Watching as a set of fingers appeared from around the other side of the door, Helen pressed herself further into the wall as they wrapped themselves around the door, they were plump in nature, opening the door wide then disappearing, Helen was not sure whether she should close the door forcefully on the fingers that had emerged from behind the door. Hearing the sound of a match being lit, after a moment of confusion mixed with the sense of danger coming, Helen watched as a bottle bomb, with the glow of the rag of fabric a light rolled along the floor.

Helen couldn't help herself freeze, watching as the flame made easy work of the rag, the glow from the fire emitting so much heat that Helen could feel the heat of the fire through her scarf. There was enough flame to light up most of the room plunging the rest of it into deeper darkness. Helen's next actions would either cause her death or save her life.

Kicking the bottle away from her, Helen thought fast, grabbed some more evidence, and flew out of the door, realising she still had much of her face hidden. Helen planned to hide in the alley until the emergency services arrived. She would disappear in the flurry of people.

Running down the stairs she could hear people outside shouting to each other in disbelief, some people were even asking if anyone was in there. Helen was, but she couldn't raise attention to herself as she shouldn't have been inside in the first place.

Through the hall, Helen counted on the fact that the people outside would be too busy looking up to notice her running out of a side gate. She hadn't been seen entering the building. Stopping once she'd exited the structure. Helen needed to slow down. If she ambled, she wouldn't be noticed. Removing her scarf from her face and readjusting her hat to get a breath of fresh air, she walked briskly away from the building and onto the street, not once looking up at the fire.

Pulling the scarf back around her face, this time over her eyes, she found herself outside the building and disappearing from view as people started to congregate in disbelief. Helen only stopped when she was in an enclave of the alleyway adjacent to the house. The wall was cold and damp, but Helen was safe to take stock of what had happened. She was safe to watch the fire. Helen was safe to think.

She watched as flames had burst through the window and was licking the paint off the windowsill above. Helen stood and watched, all the while pondering what the desired effect was of setting Grace's flat ablaze. Helen felt an overwhelming sense of fear as she considered why whoever killed Grace felt the need to kill her as well.

Helen's skin turned cold as the realisation of what could have been the consequences of her reckless behaviour consumed her every thought. For a moment, her body had become ice-like, making it hard to breathe or think straight on what to do now. Helen asked herself the question, as people pushed past her, almost knocking her to the floor, shaking herself back to reality.

Helen strolled from there onwards to home, with her head down, focusing on her breathing, which had become rapid and shallow after the sudden need to escape the flames – she had almost died. Now her body waned as she endeavoured to calm down. It would be extremely late by the time she got home, but her home wasn't on fire, and she'd be able to gain some clarity in her chores to reflect what this means for the case.

Once at the Ellentons,' Helen went straight to her room. Filling up the sink with hot water and rubbing her hands in soap, Helen began washing her face, watching as black water droplets formed and fell back into the basin. There was a knock on her door. Helen closed her eyes, all she wanted was some peace and a few minutes to collect herself before she did the last chores of the day. Couldn't she have a few minutes to herself?

'Come in,' Helen called out, a little puzzled at who it was, and whether they'd seen her rush into the house. Drying her face with her towel, trying desperately not to let her lip quiver with the tears that had formed in her eyes rolling down her cheek as Miss Henderson's plump frame did its best to curl itself around the door.

'Are you okay, Mrs Squireton, you seemed a little flushed just now as you walked in? You've been like that for a few days now, come to think of it,' Miss Henderson, asked with a quizzical look on her rounded, red face.

'Yes, Miss Henderson, I'm quite fine,' Helen replied, quite relieved, that by the sounds of things, Miss Henderson hadn't noticed the black smudges on her face.

'All right then, let me know if you need any honey in warm milk. That always calms me down after a long day,' Miss Henderson commented as she closed Helen's door. Shifting her substantial weight across the wood landing, Helen could hear the wood moan as she walked down the stairs calling orders to the maids, and cook's assistant.

There was never any risk of Miss Henderson gossiping like the maids. Still, nevertheless, Helen often wondered on what Miss Henderson's life was like before the Ellentons. She had been here long before Helen arrived and was as much a part of the house than any of the furniture.

Taking a staggered breath, Helen sat down to write what had happened in her notes. The fire, the unread evidence, and a description of the fingers, noting that the person was stoutly set.

After writing in her notes about the day's events and reminding herself that she had valuable evidence she had yet to look at thoroughly and that is what she needed to do. She stashed them safely away in one of her drawers.

The next morning, Helen set about her usual duties, polishing the silverware, and organising the ledgers along with

Mr Benton, trying to ignore anything that may make her remember about the bottle bomb, until it was time to set her uniform back in her wardrobe and set about going to bed.

That night she found herself unable to sleep. Images of attending her own funeral mixed with the flames in Grace's apartment spun around her head, punctuated with the odd picture of Benjamin. Would he have known it was her in the apartment when the Ellentons' ring, to inform the police of Helen not showing up for work. Would he be disappointed, and at the thought of Grace not getting her justice, would Benjamin let the case fall or would he continue with the case, for her?

The next day, Helen tried not to look too hard at the fire as she resumed morning briefing. She nodded at Mr Benton as he'd stepped aside to do her part of the briefing.

'As you already know by now, the guests have extended their visit with the Ellentons. Obviously, this would mean that the extra duties Mr Benton and I have assigned you still stand. I understand that this has had a strain on all of us and has made it harder to run things as smoothly as we all would like, but let's keep with it and make sure the visitors have a pleasant visit.' Helen continued to go over confirming the staff's new roles. Every time she moved the faint whiff of fuel and smoke clung to her clothes still, even after opening her window and hanging her uniform nearby to try and air out some of the smoke.

She shifted as she stood for the morning briefing, anxious to start her chores, they were the only thing keeping her distracted from the flames. She couldn't help but notice the roaring fires in the kitchen, a force of habit Helen told herself. Usually, Helen regularly took solace in the flames dancing about. Not this morning. This morning it brought back memories of the bottle bomb rolling into Grace's room, something so simple, yet it caused so much damage Helen thought as she stacked the dishes and sorted out the breakfast menu with Miss Henderson. Without warning, Helen began to wonder why whoever it was who had thrown the bottle bomb into Grace's apartment used fire. It made sense to get rid of the evidence. If someone wanted Helen dead, why not poison her like they did with Grace, they knew it worked. Helen was about the same size as Grace, both poison and fire had the desired effect, but with poison, you would only need a little, but a fire would cause maximum damage.

As she set about helping the newer maids with their duties in the kitchen, there was a clash of pots and pans being thrown into the sink. Helen jumped out of her skin, the sound brought back the image of the bottle bomb that could have killed her, or at least put her in the hospital. There would be no hiding it, and she would have to give up the investigation.

Taking a moment to collect herself again before continuing with the rest of her duties. She quietly allowed herself to sway just a little to prevent herself from shaking or crying.

Knowing very well that she was in no state to read the letters today, Helen gathered all the strength she had just to get through her jobs. Then she could leave to see Benjamin about what she had found and then she was one step closer to catching Grace's killer.

Distracting herself with service, she carried the silver bowl with a hard-boiled egg for each of the family members wrapped in muslin to keep them warm. One by one she lowered the eggs into the egg holders, paying extra attention this morning not to let her hands shake. Working her way around the family. Mr, and Mrs Ellenton first then the children who were arguing about something before the nanny hushed them and straightened out their clothes. Helen could hear tutting and sighing as Mr Ellenton lifted the freshly made tea to his lips.

'What's wrong, darling?' Mrs Ellenton asked sweetly reaching out to touch her husband's arm. Blurry eyed, she was concerned that her husband should start the day in a bad mood.

'It's the accommodation down near the market, dear. There's been a fire at one of the flats, the fire brigade wasn't called in time to save the apartment above it. Someone almost died, and they have to fix two apartments, as I can't see how the one above the one that was actually on fire would be sound,' Mr Ellenton replied, clearly not impressed at the time it had taken to phone the emergency services.

'Ah, well at least no one died,' Mrs Ellenton said, relaxing and she resumed enjoying her breakfast, satisfied that it wasn't something that would play on her husband's mind for too long.

Helen thought back on that afternoon, how quickly it could have ended so much worse. A shot of guilt went through her, her muscles in her arms and back tensed as she could feel her muscles begin to shudder. Mr Benton was watching her. Hoping that he hadn't noticed her unusual skittishness, she exited the dining room, back into the kitchen.

Guilt encased Helen, as the images of flames danced behind her smoked dry eyes. Another person almost died, and that would have been her fault. She wasn't supposed to be there.

Chapter 17

It was time for Helen to get ready to meet up with Benjamin again. She had to tell him about the love letters she'd found in Grace's flat, wondering how she would tell him, for she knew that he wouldn't be best pleased with her. It had proved to be a dangerous situation, and he had warned her against doing anything dangerous without him being there. Helen made her way to her wardrobe, flinging open her wardrobe doors, and peeling back her work clothes to reveal the three casual dresses allowed her. There was the navy and white lace one she had already worn out with Benjamin. There was a more straightforward lilac dress.

Pulling it out of her wardrobe, Helen hoped Benjamin would see that although what she did last night was a reckless thing to do, it meant she now had those letters from a mysterious Mr B. Was it worth nearly dying for? Helen couldn't decide. She would have to see whether the letters gave anything away, or if they proved any theories Helen had? She hoped he would focus more on the value of the evidence that she'd gained over the potential danger she was in – she was still alive.

Her mind poured over the letters she had on her desk from Mr B. Helen thought of names with the letter 'B;' Benjamin, no, that would mean that Deputy James could be a suspect. Helen shook at the idea; he cared too much about the case being solved.

There was something about how Deputy James had pursued this case, despite Detective Arthur's lack of belief that it was a murder case. For he was still holding on to the accidental death enquiries that intruded Helen. He may not agree with Detective Arthur's actions, still, he was very loyal to him. Would he turn criminal?

Helen didn't think he would, he respected and admired Detective Arthur too much to turn his back on him and the job. However, because of his experience as a police officer, if Benjamin were to cross the line, he would make a good criminal. Is it so much of a stretch to believe that he would stop at addressing them? Benjamin was a street boy once; he was no doubt capable.

Helen cast that name off the list and wracked her brain for anymore, none of them fitted in with the case, there was no Bernard connected to the situation or Benedict.

Realising that her current train of thought would not get her anywhere, she would go through all the names she could think that were vaguely connected to the case beginning with B, hoping to find who killed Grace. Did she expect to find her perpetrator that way? What if B was shorthand or a pet name Grace used for this man? Which changed the options a bit. Helen's last thoughts as she made her way to where Benjamin had picked her up, last time they went out together.

'I thought we could walk through the park, Helen. To work up an appetite,' Benjamin suggested as he picked her up, offering her his arm.

'Yes, Benjamin, that's a lovely idea,' Helen concurred. Going through town, even in a cab would have meant seeing the building where Grace's apartment was, and potentially revoking unpleasant memories of the night before. If Benjamin didn't know where she was last night, Helen's body shrank at the idea of keeping it from him, there would be no way for her to hide the shock and the memory from him.

Walking to the park there stood a paperboy selling newspapers to the passers-by. Helen's stomach turned as they walked past the boy, looking at the photograph on the front-page news. Helen hung on to Benjamin a little tighter as she thought about what she would do if Benjamin had figured out that she had been in Grace's apartment. Helen worried as she hoped that Benjamin didn't see or feel her body tense and then relax. If he did, he never let on that he'd noticed.

On entering the park, Helen took a small, quiet breath of relief. To her it looked as if Benjamin hadn't noticed her reaction to the image on the newspaper. As they walked along the frost encased path the grass either side of the gravel path, the sun had died down and whatever frost had remained from the early morning dew had reclaimed the earth. Their feet made a satisfying crunch as their shoes broke the thin frost on the path, breaking the silence in the otherwise quiet park.

'Do you have anything to do with that fire last night, Helen?' Benjamin asked.

Helen could feel her heart sink in her chest, then her heartbeat rose, as her chest tightened. She didn't want to lie to him, but she knew he would not be happy if she told him the truth about where she was last night. Helen thought about what to say, running through any half-truths that could be a plausible answer for him, wrestling with herself in her mind with all the satisfactory answers until she finally settled on:

'You mean to say, was I there, Benjamin?' Helen asked with a questioning tone. Benjamin slowed down and looked at her, his face filled with disappointment at her reckless actions. He listened as Helen went on.

'I thought you wanted me to help you solve the case, so why are you asking?' Helen continued. Helen was questioning him on why this line of conversation.

'So you were, you need to stop doing this, Helen. What do you think will happen if you carry on like this? If you don't stop getting yourself into trouble, particularly as this is an open investigation, I'll have to close the case, and Grace won't get her justice. I know that's what you want, I want that too, but I can't help you if you keep putting your life on the line.' Benjamin argued.

Helen was about to tell Benjamin about the letters she'd found and the bottle bomb that had all but destroyed Grace's flat when she saw Mr Hexham walking with a woman his age on his arm. Much closer to Mr Hexham than Helen was to Benjamin.

As the two couples passed, Helen heard the woman on Mr Hexham's arm speak. 'Are you sure you're all right, darling, you don't look well,' she said in a worried, slightly pandering tone.

The woman was right. Mr Hexham did not look well at all, and he still had his black armband wrapped around the top of his arm.

'Yes, dear, I'm fine, please don't worry about me,' Mr Hexham replied, sounding as tired and unwell as he looked.

'Okay, Bill, just promise me you'll take it easy at work tomorrow.

Bill, that's it, Mr Hexham is B. Helen's revelation shone through her.

'Helen, are you all right?' Benjamin asked, worried at Helen's change of pace, knocking Helen back into the real world a little.

'Mr Hexham is B,' Helen stated absent-mindedly.

Benjamin turned to face her, gently lifting her face to his. 'You have to stop this, Helen, you'll get hurt or worse.' His blatant care of her filled Helen with butterflies. Taking a breath and pulling her face away, she needed to be careful not to lose her head for she had a young woman's justice to ensure.

'Yes, Benjamin, I'm fine. I've just put some things together about the case, that is all.'

'What have you put together, Helen, come, let's sit down.' Benjamin spoke with a softer tone. Reaching into her satchel Helen pulled out the love letters found in Grace's flat.

'I found these in Grace's flat, they're love letters for the most part, I believe these could be from Mr Hexham, and I believe that the woman with him is his wife who has just called him Bill, which could be the Mr B I am looking for.'

Benjamin nodded as he flicked through them while Helen continued:

'There was another letter which was colder in tone, I have that one here,' Helen handed the letter to Benjamin. 'We don't know who this Mr B is that wrote this letter, but as we know Henry is American what's to say it's not Henry under a different name.'

'Nothing, Helen,' Benjamin simply replied, then paused while he placed the letters in his jacket pocket. 'I'll take these to the station after I drop you off, to keep them safe, but next time you want to chase a lead, you must at least tell me. First, I don't want you getting hurt.' Helen changed the topic to where they were going to eat, not wanting to agree with what he'd said out loud.

Having decided to go to the new Italian restaurant for food, and ordering their meals, Helen couldn't help her mind wandering in the moments of silence between conversation to how she didn't put Mr Hexham and Grace together, in such a way other than what would be expected from an employer-employee connection.

'I should have seen it sooner, why didn't I see it, it's so obvious.' She spoke aloud, facing Benjamin, as if she was questioning him, frustrated that her observation skills may have missed a crucial aspect of the dynamics between one of the suspects and the victim. All that time had been wasted, Helen thought, stabbing some pasta with her fork, highlighting her frustration. Wafts of warm air filled the restaurant as the waiters came in and out of the kitchen, dishes and drinks balanced carefully on their hands, sometimes even on their arms.

'How about, next time I'm off shift, we'll have a drink and go over it all together, as a whole, and see where we need to go next,' Benjamin suggested, placing an understanding hand on hers.

'Yes, that would be a great help,' Helen agreed, apologetically. Putting it to bed for now, she set herself ready to enjoy her evening out.

The evening moved on quickly as the two of them drank and enjoyed each other's company. As the restaurant went through is natural rhythm of quiet times and loud, cramped times, Helen barely noticed the time passing. The two of them found a natural rhythm of conversation.

They chatted as they drank and ate their pasta dishes, while smells of oregano, tomato, pasta, and wine, filled the air. All the while, the case was never far from Helen's mind.

'Have you been able to find any members of Grace's family, Benjamin? They ought to know that Grace has died?' Helen asked.

'You can't switch it off, can you, Helen?' Benjamin joked, smiling at her through his drink.

'No, Benjamin, I can't, we've not got anywhere in solving the case,' Helen replied, stabbing more pasta.

Benjamin nodded; he knew she had a point. Detective Arthur had closed the case, and it was just the two of them now.

'No, Helen, not yet it looks like we're not going to which is unusual but given the back-and-forth nature that you and Detective Arthur are doing, that's no surprise.'

Helen sighed again as she took a sip of her drink.

'You'll get the person who did this, Helen, I'm sure of it,' Benjamin said as he finished his meal.

Once they were both done, Benjamin went and paid, leaving Helen momentarily to her thoughts. She now knew Mr Hexham's name was Bill, she ran through what Bill was short for, of course, a letter signed B, the B could stand for anything. If Grace and Mr Hexham were having an affair, wouldn't they be more careful about their correspondence? Helen was speculating, there were no facts to prove that they were having an affair specifically.

'Do you want to walk back, Helen, or would you rather we take a cab?' Benjamin asked a lost Helen.

'Pardon?' Helen responded. 'Sorry, I was thinking about something,' she said looking at him. Then, realising she'd been caught thinking about the case again, looked down at her hands with a smile on her face, as her cheeks blushed red.

'We'll go through the park, that way you'll have more time to think things over,' Benjamin chuckled at her as they made their way first to the park, then set off back into town. As they did so, Helen thought about the letters in Benjamin's jacket.

'Benjamin, now that I've shown you the letters, can I use them to question Mr Hexham about having an affair with Grace?' Helen asked. 'I want to see how he responds. I think it'll be best if I do that myself.'

'Okay, Helen, yes, you can but once you're done, they come straight to me, agreed?' Benjamin replied.

'Agreed.' Helen felt relieved as Benjamin gave them back to her with a kiss on the side of her face. They made their way home.

Helen couldn't help but smile as she removed her shawl and placed it over her arm. It would be boiling in the kitchen, and she'd need to get to bed quickly if she were to rise early in the morning – she had leads to chase.

Chapter 18

Once again, Helen found herself with a rare day off. Today she could make some real headway in the case. She had the entire day to work on it, making sure the evidence was valid and the information was correct, even if it took her all day, which she had planned for it to do.

She collected her thoughts about the case, to see the questions that still needed answering and to develop a sense of what direction Benjamin and herself would need to take their investigation, not wanting to be the reason he got into trouble with Detective Arthur. She sat at her desk with her notes.

She detailed the murder and speculated cause of death, describing the theory on when and where the action may have occurred. And the ways someone could administer it. After Helen had completed those notes, she pulled out some other pieces of plain paper, beginning to create a detailed list of suspects she thought could be behind Grace's death. Settling on the idea that she would start with Henry Boston, as he was the most obvious suspect.

Henry Boston is the owner of the suspected crime scene. the Locus Nectar. He was acting oddly towards Helen when Grace's name was used, and the receptionist, Helen now knew goes by Mary, is around, he also speaks with an American accent now and then. Nobody seemed to know much about Henry's life before he set up his business. Though the use of

American idioms was becoming more commonplace, there was something about the frequency that they showed up in Henry's vocabulary that Helen couldn't explain away, other than Henry may not be British by birth or upbringing. Could he, in fact, could be a stranger, is he who he says he is? Helen wrote all this in her notes, pondering on the troubling fact that there was a stranger somehow tied up in a random murder, a local and much-loved bartender who was so familiar. Yet he was a stranger, she knew nothing much about him.

This led Helen to think about the receptionist Helen now knew was called Mary. Helen also knew that one connection between Mary and Grace was that they worked together. That was all Helen knew. What reason would there be for Mary to kill Grace? Helen couldn't help but notice how Mary's demeanour had changed from when Mary first saw Helen at Mr Hexham's to when she was at the Locus Nectar talking to Henry. She tried to piece together a plausible series of scenarios how such a young woman such as Mary could get herself tied up in so much mess. Helen wondered as she took a break, flexing her fingers out as her muscles had ached with the speed she was writing. Helen thought there could be an element of an unwitting accomplice. So, no real motivation on Mary's part to killing her work colleague. Somehow Helen thought that unlikely, as though Mary wasn't too young to be capable of murder if she did have a hand in this, and Helen suspected she did so, could she be involved at the will of someone else. Mary was someone else's puppet, another person was pulling at her strings, manipulating her to be a pawn in their game of catch me if you can. Helen would find them, she had to. For Grace.

Mary must still be a woman of some education to be a

receptionist at a legal firm. This led Helen to think there must be something deep down about Grace, that Mary didn't like to enable whoever wanted Grace dead to be able to manipulate Mary to be their accomplice.

Helen thought of the times where she'd seen Mary enter the Locus Nectar to speak to Henry. There was something about the way Mary left the Locus Nectar when Helen was about to walk past. There was a connection between Mary and Henry. Was it Mary who had access to strychnine? Henry brewed his own beer for the bar from time to time, but there needed to be a reason why they had teamed up to kill Grace. Helen's pen scratching the paper was the only noise in the room. With the sounds of pots being placed on the stove and plates clashing trying to seep into Helen's mind, but to no avail, Helen was too focused on what she was doing to even think about the outside world.

Finally, the last suspect, Mr Hexham. What is his connection to Grace? He's her employer at face value, what if he's more than just her employer, or rather ex-employer? Helen noted that if there was a love connection to Grace, then where is the motivation to kill her? A jilted lover could be a motivation, Helen thought, but remembering Mr Hexham's demeanour, she didn't think him the jealous type, however, Helen kept circling back to the grief that still lingered around Mr Hexham like a moth to a flame. She needed to find out why,

That's when Helen remembered the letters that she had found in Grace's apartment; they were of a dubious nature to be from an employer. Mr Hexham's wife did call him Bill. Helen knew this was to be her next action, to see what Mr Hexham has to say about these letters.

A feeling of determination came over Helen, mixed with

relief. Judging from the conversation her and Benjamin had had together on their evening out, Helen knew she had finally got him on her side. Even if he wasn't willing to talk about the case with her much, the case was beginning to uncover secrets that would lead to Grace's killer coming to justice. Helen was sure of it.

Sitting back in her seat for a moment, it was time for offices and businesses to open. Helen took a moment to quell her frustration at how little information she had before she continued pinning down the links each one had to Grace and the murder. She gave them each their own piece of paper in case any new information would need to be added as she put the case together.

Walking into the solicitor's, Helen noted that Mary wasn't the one at the desk, and Mr Hexham was out of his office filing paperwork himself. Noticing Mary's absence from the front desk, Helen began to speculate why she wasn't at work that day. Furthermore, Helen realised that the front desk had been cleared of all Mary's personal items. When Helen first arrived at the solicitor's, she'd noticed that Mary's desk had a picture frame angled so that it was nearest to Mary in such a way that she'd have been able to see it without much movement. Or having to break her focus to look at it. Then there was the disappearance of the cactus on her desk.

Turning her attention back to Mr Hexham, Helen couldn't help but notice he still wore his black armband at work. This time he made no attempt to conceal it from people she wondered whether Mr Hexham should have stayed at home rather than come to work. However, that could arouse suspicion as he still had a business to run, and Grace was merely an employee, nothing more, to everyone else, at least.

'Mr Hexham, could I trouble you for a moment of your

time?' Helen asked, mindful that he was taking Grace's death more to heart than usual, still grieving and he hadn't put anything up on the window about there being a vacancy. Helen thought this odd as one of the times he'd dismissed her from his office he'd mentioned having applications to shortlist, yet there was no vacancy sign up, and it was evident by the lack of a receptionist at the front desk the position hadn't been filled.

'Yes, Miss Squireton, come on through, I'll just be a moment, wait in my office if you would.' He naturally sounding better than he felt, rolling back his shoulders while taking a deep breath, he then wiped away a tear in his eye.

Sat waiting for Mr Hexham, Helen had noticed the rat poison had gone from the edges of the room. Helen couldn't help but think the look and the timing of the rat poison felt a bit suspicious. Mr Hexham entered; the little regained colour had drained away from his face. Helen carefully pulled the letters she had found in Grace's apartment. She puzzled over how to ask Mr Hexham about them but saw he had already spotted them.

'Are they for me, Miss Squireton?' Mr Hexham asked, closing the door behind him. Helen wondered how to proceed.

'They seem to be from you, Mr Hexham, I've looked through them.' Helen paused to allow Mr Hexham's reaction to show, he had begun to lose his composure as another wave of loss hit him. 'You and Grace had embarked on an affair, shortly before she was killed. I'm sorry to ask, but is this true?'

Mr Hexham sighed, still standing near the door as he was lowering the blinds.

'Yes, Miss Squireton, we did have an affair but not for a while,' Mr Hexham answered, overcome with grief, barely making it to the chair behind his desk. 'She was so beautiful, my Gracie, my wife must never know, you must not tell her. I've already lost one love; I don't wish to lose another. I would never kill Grace.'

Helen offered him her handkerchief as he sobbed, repeating Grace's name over and over again. 'You must believe me, Miss Squireton, I loved her.'

Helen sighed. 'I'm sorry for your loss. You must think this an impertinence, but how long did this affair last?' Helen asked gently showing the letters to Mr Hexham.

'We were together just under six months before she broke it off. I know, jilted lover, the perfect suspect but I was happy to admire her from afar, the one that got away,' Mr Hexham answered, as he caressed the letters he had written to her.

'Here I have some proof it wasn't me,' he said, stifling tears as he pulled out a letter. 'It explains how I felt about her and that I'd come to terms with her not wanting me.' He was tearing up again as he sorted out the letters ready to wrap in his armband. Helen watched the elderly man as he swept his hand over them. His face contorted, showing some sort of confusion. Before Helen could ask what was wrong, Mr Hexham voiced his answer. 'This isn't from me, it's not my handwriting, and I had no need to disguise my handwriting in her letters. Grace and I were always meticulous not to get caught.'

Mr Hexham handed the unrelated letter back to Helen for inspection. He was right they were different, both in handwriting and in tone, this letter was more of a note, and it read:

You must not contact me now, Grace. I am going away, do not speak to me ever again, it is over.

Then signed:

B.

Putting it back into her handbag, Helen thanked Mr Hexham for his time and once again apologised to him for the pain caused.

'Just get who did this, Miss Squireton, and then I can grieve in peace.' Sat in his armchair, the grieving Mr Hexham looked more like a lost boy than a well put together businessman.

Helen nodded as she placed her hand on the door and made her way to leave Mr Hexham in peace.

Chapter 19

Helen made her way towards the Ellentons,' cutting through the busy marketplace to grab some daily required goods. Once she was done in the market, she planned to spend a few minutes in her room to write up some thoughts in her notes.

They had three suspects, all with the opportunity to kill her. Henry could have administered the poison at the bar, and both Mary and Mr Hexham could have poisoned Grace at work. However, the clothing that Grace was wearing when Helen bumped into Grace, she wasn't wearing work clothes, they were more casual wear, making Helen lean towards the idea that she had, in fact, been at the Locus Nectar that fateful Friday. Helen knew it was time to check in with Benjamin again. She had even more questions to answer. What was the connection between Henry and Mary? What drove them to commit or get involved in killing Grace? And if it was, in fact, Mr Hexham then how did he dose Grace with the poison?

She wandered through the market, taking in the smells of the spices and exotic fruits that had been brought from the new world. Walking down the more substantial pedestrian entrance to the market, Helen was relieved that although there was a lot of foot traffic, everybody had kept moving at a pace that allowed the flow of movement to be steady and not congested. She peeked through some ventilated holes in the wall, to where the merchants' carts would be. All was still apart from a few people using it as a shortcut back out of the market.

She picked up one fruit, and felt the smooth skin, checking the quality of the ingredients. While Helen was finishing up in the market, her hamper almost full, her spine tingled, and her ears seemed to have peeled back as adrenaline crept up her spine then down her arms and legs. She was being watched, and she couldn't see who by.

She stopped to take stock of the situation without creating a scene, neither did she want to alert whoever it was, that she had noticed that they were watching her, if it was indeed her they were watching.

Shaking it off, she continued with the chores, chalking it up to it being paranoia about the person who threw a bottle bomb into Grace's apartment the other night.

Moving on to a stall with a wide variety of vegetables such as beetroot, pumpkins and a variety of squashes, Helen looked for the ingredients she would need for the following day. Even if it was her day off today, there was still time-sensitive jobs to do that couldn't wait until tomorrow.

Gathering the last few things on her list, Helen readjusted her hamper on her arm flexing her elbow while she did so, for the pain in her arm had become too much to just ignore. As she went to stall after stall Helen found there was less and less of what she needed.

'Sorry, miss, we've run out of beetroot for this week, it seems to be growing in popularity these days,' a stall owner replied to Helen's request. 'I can keep some aside for you next week, just tell me how much you need.'

'That's okay. For now, I'll take these.' Helen smiled and nodded as she had her back-up plan to have the proper ingredients for what was in season as well as what meals she knew the family would enjoy.

Helen noticed the shadowy figure leaning against the archway in the pedestrian entrance to the market. Helen saw that it was a man of stocky build who was well used to working in shadows. She couldn't decipher what he was looking at, there were lots of people around, but he remained still as if whatever he was watching was still in his line of sight. The figure remained relaxed as Helen lifted the produce from the baskets and placed them into her hamper.

She paid closer attention to the figure, trying to see who they were and did she know them. She didn't recognise anything about him, but she could have sworn she'd seen him before. As her heart rate increased and the hairs on the back of her neck stood upright and rigid, she knew she had to move. Helen didn't want him to get too close, something about him was dangerous, that much she knew. Helen wondered whether he was watching her. If so, could she bring him out of hiding and into the light?

After a few minutes of ducking around stalls and in between people, it was quite clear the man did not want to be seen. Helen couldn't help the hair on the back of her neck pick up as she wondered what exactly the man was trying to accomplish. She had started to look for any distinguishing features on the man, ready to give to Benjamin discreetly for it followed some sort of logic that he could be connected to one of the suspects in the murder.

Helen walked further into the market, watching the figure's reaction. Moving slightly, the figure was unsure of the best course of action to take, making it even harder for Helen to have a good look at him and to figure out what it was about him that made her feel uneasy.

Helen stopped for a little, trying to read the situation as

best as possible. The figure was definitely uncomfortable, even agitated, when she moved out of his line of sight. Helen couldn't shake the feeling the man was watching her. However, all she had was her gut and speculation. As she stood still, he settled back into the shadows. His relief was noticeable, even from where Helen stood, adding to Helen's sense of pressure – of fear. Her muscles in her back had begun to twinge as the adrenaline still had hold of her, and she was unbalanced with her hamper pulling at her arm. She needed to get away to confirm her hunch.

Settling her sense of fear, Helen decided to carry on with her day, reminding herself that it would be a bad idea to cause a scene when all her feelings were based on speculation. She had no proof that the man following her had any malice in following her. It was merely a hunch. She began to wonder if her suspicion about this being connected to what she was doing about Grace's death, was more like paranoia. Then Helen remembered that if someone wanted someone to disappear, there were other, better ways of making that happen.

Not long after, Helen thought she had shaken him off, or boredom had set in. Did he know where she was headed so knew he had limited time on his hands to harm her? When she felt someone with an iron grip grab her around the chest.

Pulling her into a more shaded area, she felt a hand round her face and a silk handkerchief smothering her nose and mouth. She tried to escape, kicking and scratching at the man. She knew she had become too lax in being watchful for the figure who she'd seen grow agitated at her attempts to hide from him. He had her in his grasp, and there was no means of escape.

Once the reality kicked in that, he wasn't beating her.

confusion engulfed her. What was he trying to achieve? That's when she noticed the sweet smell of the handkerchief, she had over her face. Helen tried to fight the dizziness she was beginning to feel. She grabbed his hand to attempt to remove the silk and breathe some uncontaminated air. Her attacker just gripped her chest tighter, and Helen could barely think straight as she struggled with him, thrashing at him with every part of her that was loose. Her attacker didn't flinch. He'd been doing this for a while – an expert. Helen could feel the way he held her close to him with one arm and squeezed all the air from her with the other.

Feeling her eyes begin to grow weary and start to close, Helen told herself she was not going to let this man beat her. She began to find the energy to continue to fight and develop some sort of plan, any plan to get herself out of this man's grasp and be able to breathe. Helen tried to fight her assailant off, tearing at him as she felt for a part of him she could get a grip of and wriggle her way out of the mess she was in.

Between attempts at fighting for herself, she saw people walking by, not able to notice her in the sideway. Helen tried to scream, but he would only put the handkerchief further into her mouth. Helen wanted to bite it in the hope of getting his finger caught in her teeth, but all she got was silk. Before long, it was wet with saliva.

Helen wondered if she could play dead, that would make her attacker leave her alone. Willing herself to breathe, determined to get this man away from her, Helen fought off the weariness in her eyes for she knew this was the time to see if there was anything she recognised about who it was. That's if Helen knew him, this would be the situation when she could find out, if she could keep her eyes open.

Taking a shallow breath so as to not let whatever was on the handkerchief knock her unconscious, Helen acted.

Letting herself go limp, Helen could feel his grip loosen, her plan was working so far. He left her lying in the gutter as Helen fought the urge to resist him. Helen heard a loud call from somewhere in the distance and a carthorse neighing loudly. Whoever it was called out to her attacker to leave her alone. Kicking her a little too hard to the kerb, her attacker warned her with a low grunt. 'Don't be stupid, or I'll leave you in the trash.' Helen heard the sound of her attacker's feet run away from her and fade from the distance. It had been Henry who'd attacked her, in broad daylight.

With the knowledge that she was now free from his grasp, and with the pain from being squeezed too hard, Helen finally let her eyes close as the smell of whatever was on the silk handkerchief cleared from her nose and mouth and the pain slowly ebbed away. She fell into some sort of deep, dreamless sleep.

Opening her eyes as someone had begun to shake her awake, Helen felt her eyes shut automatically for a moment as the brightness of the sun proved too much for her to take in as a dry feeling engulfed her mouth. Taking a moment as her eyes adjusted to the sun again, blinking slowly, Helen could hear a voice, first muffled, then clear. She began to look around as she tried to recall who it was. Helen decided to sit up, the feeling of dizziness came over her. It was the stall owner as he helped her sit up against the archway wall.

'How long have I been unconscious for?' Helen asked, trying to breathe steadily as she tried to regain some sense of strength.

'A good few minutes, miss, are you okay. The missus

won't be best pleased if I'm late for lunch,' the stall owner asked, almost asking for Helen's permission to leave her. Helen knew she wasn't really in a fit state to walk home on her own. Neither did she want to let the stall owner get into trouble for showing some common courtesy and kindness. Pushing herself up on her feet, she knew she could make it back home if she took it slowly and didn't take any detours or stopped. She would be fine. Once she was home, she would be safe.

Standing slowly, she collected her hamper from him. 'Thank you, very much. I'll be fine from here,' she said stifling tears and the tremors that had engulfed her body from the pain of bruised ribs and shock.

'All right, miss, take care of yourself,' the stallholder said encouragingly as he helped her to her feet and took off to go his own way but not before stopping and looking behind him to see Helen take a couple of steps towards the Ellentons' house.

Walking back home, trying not to think about the smell of his cologne or his arms around her chest. She would need to spend the day resting in her room, writing what she could recall from the event in the marketplace and decide the next course of action.

Chapter 20

With her head faced down, she picked her footing, with her arm wrapped around her waist. Breathing carefully, she tried to avoid the stabbing pain in her ribs made if she breathed too much.

Avoiding any street where Benjamin could bump into her as she weaved through town, Helen's heart slid into her stomach at the thought of what could happen to the case if Benjamin could see the state she was in. After one last turn left out of town, she had about a mile left to go. Straightening herself up as she walked the mile, legs throbbing and knees protesting as she was walking home. Getting a cab would have attracted too much attention. Rolling her shoulders every now and again, Helen pushed on. She would not be safe until she was at the Ellentons.'

Helen's heart couldn't help but sing inside as she saw the stately house, she called home. She was out of all danger for today.

Upon seeing the servant's entrance door, she summoned the energy and strength to open the door, breathing in, preparing herself for pain, and then sighing with relief as Mr Benton had seen her struggle with the door on his way out. All she had to do now was tackle the stairs up to her room.

This time it was her thighs turn to protest. She had to take her time, all the while getting frustrated with herself. She'd run up and down these stairs half asleep. It never took her this long. She moved her hand up the banister an inch then took a step, paused, then lifted the other leg to join the two of them together. She walked up the steep stairs like a toddler, not a grown woman.

He had held the door for her as Helen slid past him, her skin tingling with sensitivity at the narrow space between them. Looking up at him, she could tell he knew she was in trouble. Neither of them said anything to each other, much to Helen's salvation, as she didn't think she could hide it from Mr Benton had he asked what was wrong with her. Helen knew she couldn't mislead or outright lie to him; he would see straight past that. He never enjoyed being lied to, and Helen didn't want to lie to him.

The shock had come back with a vengeance. Putting her hand over her mouth as she closed her bedroom door, she slid down to the floor. Clasping her head in her hands, Helen sobbed, struggling to find a positive in what had happened. Her ribs wailed with pain; tears flowed down her cheeks as her breathing became rapid. Her eyes widened, her heartbeat faster and faster. Helen couldn't breathe. All Helen could smell was the handkerchief. All Helen could see through the haze of this panic attack was her attacker. All she could hear was, "Don't be stupid, or I'll leave you in the trash." All she could do was close her eyes so that she couldn't see him. Helen began to hum so she couldn't hear him, her breathing became regular but pained and her heart rate normalised.

She pulled herself together, for crying only made her ribs worse. It was time to make some notes. Helen hoped she could remember enough to be able to take some sort of action. What action, she didn't know, but one thing was for sure, she wasn't going to let what had happened to her go undocumented.

The thought of writing it down to decide what to do with it later soothed Helen. Her lips wobbled as her breathing turned to as healthy as possible with bruised ribs, as she whisked tears away from her cheeks.

Helen lifted herself off the floor, using the little furniture she had or the wall to support herself; she made her way to her desk. She pulled out a separate sheet of paper and, taking a deep breath, Helen's stubborn side began to show as she lowered herself on to the chair at her desk and began to write out an account of the event, as detailed as she could bear.

As she wrote, there were three things her mind came back to. This man was stronger than Helen had given him credit for if it wasn't Henry, Helen wondered what job her attacker may have had, it would need to be a job that required a large amount of strength, but one that didn't ask too many questions, for it was clear that her attacker knew what he was doing. There aren't many jobs that teach you how to follow and attack someone.

As for the smell of unfamiliar cologne, musky and combined with sweat, she swallowed the panic that the memory of his smell had brought back to her. Trying to be active, she carried on with her day off, enjoying the time where she didn't have any chores to do. She had no one to be responsible for, spending the rest of the afternoon either in her room or sitting on a small garden chair with a table in front of her. A cup of tea in her hands, the book she had borrowed from the library. Reading *A Scandal in Bohemia*, she began to nurse her ribs, for the shock had subsided. Helen prayed that the flashbacks would disappear in time for her to head to bed that evening.

No such luck found her as she painfully tossed and turned

in her bed as she dreamed of the incident. The smell once again filling her nostrils as vivid images of arms wrapped around her chest, and silk handkerchiefs flew around her head with their own weird, sweet smell. What was her body trying to fight? In a moment of consciousness, Helen ran through all the poisons she had seen in her father's book, searching for what the poison was on the silk handkerchief, with no luck thinking of anything.

Helen couldn't bear not knowing what it was on the handkerchief that caused her to pass out during her attack. Whatever it was smelled like some sort of ether compound. Still, when Helen bit her attacker through the scarf, the liquid tasted sweet, confusion had her grasping at straws at what it might be, and she would need to speak to the pathologist to find that out. Helen was going to make it a priority to see Benjamin tomorrow.

Being woken by throbbing pain as she had accidentally laid on her bruised ribs, Helen faced a decision. It was a given she needed to talk to Benjamin about Henry attacking her yesterday.

Helen thought about going and telling Benjamin what had happened, but then there was the problem of how he would react, he'd already asked her to stop. There was the issue of there being nothing to stop him from barring her from going any further on the case, then Grace wouldn't get her justice. Helen took a moment; she could feel her face become sour at the fact that there would be a chance of her actions forcing Benjamin dropping his offer to help her with the investigation away from Detective Arthur. Taking a breath, she surprised herself. Helen quickly thought how she could report her attack without being barred from the case, ensuring that Grace had her justice and that Helen's attacker didn't go unnoticed.

If she went to her father then he could look at her ribs and confirm whether they were bruised or broken, but then he would tell the police, and that could be misconstrued as Helen perverting the course of justice, so that was not ideal.

Finding Benjamin on duty near the entrance to the alley where Grace had fallen into her arms, Helen asked him if he wanted a drink after his shift.

'We need to talk about the case, Benjamin,' Helen explained. Though this wasn't the whole truth, it was enough to express the urgency to him.

'I'm off shift in ten minutes as it happens, I'll meet you at the Locus Nectar,' Benjamin replied, joyfully taken aback at the role reversal.

Not thinking straight due to the immense pain she was in; Helen agreed to this and slowly made her way towards town. She would nip into her father's surgery, for there would be a nurse on duty today. That way she could avoid having to tell her father anything.

After the nurse prescribed some painkillers and confirmed that Helen's ribs were bruised and not broken, Helen began the ten-minute walk to the Locus Nectar to meet with Benjamin.

The progress again was slow, but Helen felt the painkillers she had taken with the nurse had begun to kick in enough to allow her to walk straight, speeding the process up a little.

Entering the Locus Nectar once again, Helen noticed Henry's slightly shocked expression as she sat down in the darkest booth available. Helen started to wonder why the surprise. He had regularly seen her here on her days off and often smiled and waved at her. Flashbacks from last night whirled around her head, she didn't know him well. His attitude had significantly changed towards her. Fear hit Helen hard as her ribs and arms twitched painfully. Remembering her ordeal, Helen wondered if he knew something about last night, or even who attacked her. She didn't want to draw attention to her pain while she waited for Benjamin to arrive. As she sat there, she couldn't help but play with her fingers, a bad, unladylike habit that Helen had tried to stop time and time again. Extenuating circumstances, she told herself, then shook her head as she sat on her hands for a moment while she calmed herself down.

In a brief moment of tiredness, Helen gently leaned against the glass when she heard Henry once again talk to someone on the phone.

'Time to take out the garbage.' Henry was threatening someone, hints of an American accent, thoroughly disguised, seeping through his words.

As Helen listened more closely, she realised the situation she was in, she was in a potential crime scene, waiting for Benjamin, who had not arrived yet, with one of her suspects. Knowing full well that she looked like a sitting duck, Helen summoned all her strength, she could not look like a victim. Straightening herself up, trying to look as though the beating hadn't affected her, either the mental trauma or the physical trauma, Helen did everything she could to establish herself as stable and with it as possible, at least till Benjamin arrived.

Just then, Benjamin slid into the booth.

'I couldn't see you for a moment there, are you all right, Helen?' Benjamin asked, taking in the well-hidden but pained expression on her face.

Helen's mouth twitched, she knew she wanted to tell him and tell him everything. The case, the attack, even about the cologne, but would he talk to Detective Arthur and bar her from continuing on the path she had taken. 'If I tell you, then you'll just be mad.' Please don't be angry, Helen thought as she looked across at him, pain evident on her face. Still not sure that telling him was the best thing to do, even if it meant Benjamin being mad at her, she could always argue her case, she had the evidence on her desk in her room.

'I'm telling you this as a civilian, not as a police officer,' Helen blurted out with a mix of fear and pain then, when the pain in her ribs got too much to bear, whingeing in pain.

'It's okay, Helen, I won't tell if you don't want me to. What happened to you?' It was Benjamin's turn to hide what he was feeling, but reached for Helen's hand, giving away his concern for her. Helen moved her hand away from his sharply. Confusion showed on his face, she would have let him touch her if it wasn't for her skin being particularly sore on this occasion.

'I was attacked last night, Benjamin, by Henry, I think it's to do with Grace Andrew's murder,' Helen said, stiffening her pain with the sudden movement.

Chapter 21

'You mean to say that, despite me telling you to stop, you carried on anyway, oh Helen!' Benjamin's concern changed to dismay. 'What am I going to do with you?' Tears filled Helen's eyes; she wrote on a napkin as she did so.

Helen handed the napkin with a more detailed description of what had happened to him. She couldn't bear going into detail out loud, for if it was the case that Henry had something to do with her attack, then Helen didn't want to alert him. Neither did she want to face that what had happened was real, and her fault.

Benjamin's demeanour changed to that of a bear, but he remained almost professional in tone. 'Okay, I'll pay for your drink, you leave and meet me at the back, I'll go round the front, and we'll meet in the middle,' he told her in a hushed tone as Henry was walking past.

Helen found relief as Benjamin hadn't been as annoyed at her as she had thought, he could see she was in no state to be told off and needed to feel safe rather than face another fight of some description.

Helen did what she was told, waited for Benjamin to meet her in a side alleyway. Just as she had conquered her pain, she saw Mary beckon to her, mouthing, 'I know something you need to hear about Grace.'

Without a second thought about where Benjamin may be,

Helen took off after Mary the best she could while the pain in her ribs had subsided. Following every step Mary took, knowing that her current course of action would not go down well with Benjamin. Helen's curiosity got the better of her as the lure of gaining some insight on the case was too tempting for her to pass up.

As Helen followed Mary, she could see glimmers of doubt in Mary's demeanour. She would go one way, then stop and take another street, leaving Helen with the questioning what it was Mary was trying to do.

Turning down onto a narrow, isolated street, Helen told Mary, who had now become sheepish to pass on all she knew about Grace. Just then, something cold and hard struck Helen from behind. All Helen could think of then was Benjamin's face, disappointed at her, not being able to leave it alone while she recovered. Disappointment all over his face as she hit the ground with a thud. As her eyes fluttered with the impact, her bruised ribs screeched in pain. In the few moments of consciousness Helen had left as her body screamed in pain, she could see Mary's petite feet being joined by another set of feet, bigger. Helen guessed they were male. Still, she didn't recognise them. As her consciousness wavered, she willed the owner of the second set of feet to speak, but there was nothing but silence. Her body finally gave up, as she lost consciousness.

Coming round sometime later from the whack on her head, she found herself somewhere she shouldn't be for the second time in as many days.

Helen felt the cold, damp floor. Shifting slightly, she found herself in some sort of basement with a wooden hatch in the roof of the basement leading to the street above.

As she sat there bound by thick rope, Helen began to listen and watch. There were large barrels of whisky along the wall opposite her, with brewing equipment stacked high. Steadying her heartbeat, she could hear the clanging of glasses and the jolly cheer of drunken men. She was in the basement of the Locus Nectar. Helen thought fast. She knew she needed to let someone know where she was. Noticing that there was light in the street above her. She hadn't been out of it for long, which meant there would still be people outside to hear her.

She shouted, but her mouth opened only to find that rope had been tied around her mouth as well as her arms and legs.

Rolling her eyes at her luck, Helen screamed harder and began to try and bounce her way out of her bonds, making as much noise as she could to alert anybody to her presence. As she jumped, her ribs clenched at her lungs, and her mouth grew dryer and dryer as she screamed through the rope. The edge of her mouth began to redden with the rope being tied around her mouth so tight.

As she began to tire of her efforts, the door flew open and down rolled a very bloody Henry, scowling at Helen with a glare that made your hairs stand straight, followed by Benjamin with a busted lip and a torn sleeve. Helen couldn't help but snarl back.

Looking at Benjamin, Henry made for Helen, who had no energy to scream, before Benjamin dragged him by the trouser leg and pulled him into the shadows behind the barrels of what smelt like beer brewing in big, wooden barrels.

Henry dug his hands into the damp floor and tried to twist to face Benjamin, followed by Benjamin kicking him sharply. Helen watched with fear, she had never seen Benjamin like this, he no longer looked like a police officer. He was a street kid in a fight, he was out for blood. Helen spotted a piece of glass, her eyes widened as she calculated how sharp the lens would be. Making a grab for it in an instant, Helen began trying to free herself with it planning to go and get some sort of backup for Benjamin once she had released herself.

All the while, Helen could hear Benjamin and Henry coming to blows with each other. One after another, some in quick succession, some slower, it was apparent neither of them would back down.

Helen didn't have time to think about how much trouble Benjamin and herself would be in as she made little progress on the thick heavy-duty rope that bound her feet only stopping when she heard the sound of handcuffs locking into place, then silence. Helen wondered who it was who was in the cuffs, hoping that Benjamin had managed to arrest Henry and that Henry hadn't stolen his cuffs.

Shortly after, the two disgruntled men emerged from the shadows. Benjamin looked really fed up and had a tight hold of the now barely standing Henry as Benjamin dragged him up the stairs and whistled to some on-duty junior officers.

'Put him in a cell, leave him there until I come for him,' he called out.

There was a pause as the junior officers peered into the basement, sharing a look, baffled at the disgruntled and badly beaten Deputy James appeared from the basement with Henry tied up in cuffs. Not wanting to move towards Henry, until Benjamin shouted with anger, 'Do you want to lose your jobs?' There was a scuffle as the officers scrambled to take Henry off Benjamin.

The scuffle then escalated into shouting and more sounds of people coming to blows, followed by an order to catch him, given by Benjamin.

Chapter 22

Much to Helen's relief, Benjamin returned down the wooden stairs. Bloodied and with a slight limp, kneeling to untie Helen and noticing the shard of bottle glass he found in her hands, he smiled at her little chance of escape using that against the thick industrial rope Henry had used to tie her up.

'Don't, Benjamin, not now,' Helen warned him against a funny remark at the situation. Tiredness covered Helen; her head throbbed with pain again causing a wave of dizziness. Once that had passed, she could concentrate on Benjamin. She hadn't even thought of what injuries he had sustained during the scuffle with Henry.

Taking in Helen's slightly puzzled look at him having a bust lip and not being in pain, Benjamin looked at her and said, 'I used to be a street kid, remember, I've had worse done to me.'

Helen's face pulled itself to one that showed her lack of satisfaction at his answer. Looking at Helen and taking in her displeasure at his response, Benjamin shrugged his shoulders. Part of her wanted him to change his answer, neither did she want to discuss his injuries with him, she already felt guilty for putting him in harm's way.

'What happened up there, Benjamin, why all the noise?' Helen asked as he helped her up, and she dusted off her clothes as best she could.

'Henry's done a runner, Helen, the junior officers ran after him, but I doubt they'll catch him, he's too cunning to be caught again soon. We'll catch him, Helen, don't worry, he's slipped up once. He'll slip up again.'

Helen rolled her eyes as she gritted her teeth, then checked whether Benjamin had noticed her frustration once again, he never let on if he had or not as they both stood side by side for a moment, looking around the basement. They were alone, both wondering what to do next. Looking back round at Benjamin Helen could see that he was also in a bad way, her heart sank at what she had caused.

'We need to get you to the hospital, Benjamin that lip won't heal itself,' Helen suggested, seeing a smile form on his face. 'But you won't do that will you.' Helen knew she wasn't going be able to convince him to go, nor was she in any condition herself to be the one to persuade him to go.

'Not before we've given this place a good look over. There could be something here relating to the case, and how Henry has had a part in it all,' Benjamin replied.

'But you've got yourself injured, Benjamin. I don't want you making your injuries worse,' Helen said, pointing at his leg and lip. 'Let's go to the hospital and get you sorted.' Helen pointed out that there were more important things to do at that moment in time.

'Meanwhile, Henry comes back and destroys any evidence or commits another murder. He may succeed at killing you, given I'm injured.' Feeling as though that was a bit insensitive of him, she knew she would get out of the rope. She took a breath and put the lack of tact in his words down to the bruised lip and the injured leg he was hobbling about on.

'Fine, we'll do this your way,' Helen grumbled as she let

go of him to start looking for evidence. Helen was still not convinced this was the most important thing to do just now, surely herself and Benjamin could do this more quickly if their respective injures had been checked first.

Questioning Benjamin's method of prioritising, Helen began looking for evidence behind the large barrels of beer brewing, squeezing herself behind them at times. She looked at Benjamin watching her out of the corner of his eye with a concerned look on his face whenever she moved behind the barrels.

'Afraid I'll disappear again, are we?' she questioned him in a playful tone as she locked eyes with him.

'Picking on me for caring for you, are we?' came Benjamin's reply as he hobbled over to lend her a hand back out from behind the barrels. Helen laughed, for all his funny remarks may annoy her at times, she did enjoy them when he got them in at the right time.

'I'm not sure we're going to find much evidence of Grace's murder here, Benjamin, just my kidnapping,' Helen said, looking in a few more areas of the basement, avoiding the place where Henry and Benjamin had their scuffle. 'We should look elsewhere for evidence relating to the murder.' Helen half thought to give the basement one last look-over, as she dusted the muck of her clothes.

'I agree. You know the Locus Nectar better than I do, Helen. Where to next?' he said, letting her go for a moment.

Looking at him. 'You're the police officer, where do people usually hide incriminating evidence, Deputy James?' Helen replied, half mocking him.

'Somewhere close to their person, where they can get to it easily,' Benjamin replied. 'Now where would that be?' he asked, smiling at her the best he could.

Knowing that Henry wasn't due to work today, which made it unlikely it was somewhere near the front of house, Helen mused. She listened out to hear any familiar voices from the Locus Nectar above, more of the regular punters had arrived. They were sober enough to recognise her, so she couldn't search there, or at least do it quickly without being seen by any of them. Thinking about where Henry would keep incriminating evidence, she thought carefully, going through everything that she knew about him. To no avail. Helen thought where someone as secretive as Henry would keep such things. She turned her mind to Grace's apartment, all the letters and unpaid rent notices, she kept them hidden in her desk. With this, Helen finally spoke.

'I believe he lives in the flat above, and my room is where I keep my personal paperwork, so let's check there. I could check in his office, as I'm not covered in blood and have a busted lip, while you head out of the back door and enter the flat above via the stairs at the side of the building.'

She double-checked one last time that her dress was presentable, and she didn't look as if there was something untoward going on.

She made her way up out of the basement and into the side entrance, ignoring the drunken men who were beginning to rotate between standing outside for a smoke or for some fresh air and narrowly being missed by one of the bar staff. Henry has strict no admittance rules about some regions of the building, which would make the perfect hiding spots for evidence. Helen took a couple of deep breaths as her heart began to race. Both her and Benjamin knew who Grace's killer was, all they needed to do was gather the evidence to prove it and catch him, As Benjamin said, he's slipped up once, he'll slip up again.

As she entered his office, Helen's heart melted at how disorganised the place was. Loose bits of paper piled high on what Helen could only guess was supposed to be a desk. Boxes were stacked on top of one another. Nearly crying at how high the boxes were stacked, Helen's hands gently touched her ribs. She wondered how long her makeshift wrap would hold and hoped that the evidence she was looking for was in one of the boxes lower down. Helen began the search for evidence.

Ignoring any impulse to organise the place, Helen opened boxes. She scanned through papers after papers, telling herself that they were more places to look in and that meant it was okay not to find anything in his office, plus it would be a hard place to look for evidence, especially in the mess Henry kept it in.

Helen scoured the office for somewhere to start. Looking for inspiration, she began to work the room in a clockwise direction from bottom to top, leaving the harder to reach boxes to last, opening them and delving into each box she opened. After what must have been her thirtieth box, Helen could feel the temperature drop, prompting her to look at her watch. She must have spent at least an hour looking for evidence, and once again this was a dead end.

Giving up in the office, Helen made her way out of the back and up the stairs to enter Henry's flat at the top of the building. Opening the door, she saw that Benjamin had made a decent start, some drawers hadn't been pushed in all the way. It was clear that the bed had been disturbed. Helen wondered how Benjamin had managed to look under the mattress on his own, then remembered what Benjamin had said when they were downstairs about him having been in worse condition. Helen took a moment to take in the similarity of how Grace's room and Henry's room were sparsely furnished, considering neither of them was in domestic service.

While Grace's room showed that she hadn't made a home out of her apartment yet, if she ever planned to, Henry's was the opposite. Cupboards and filing cabinets cluttered the walls shelves and were filled with the meaningless clutter you develop once you've spent any amount of time in the same place. News clippings about the Locus Nectar opening for the first time hung in frames on the wall. Helen couldn't help but notice they were all old, neglected memories. The room itself felt more used and warmer than Grace's. Helen figured that it was down to time being spent in one place, for she didn't take Henry for the sentimental type. He was a high achiever, most definitely, but then why let the news clippings become dusty and neglected? Judging by the amount of dust on the glass panels, it was a couple of months at least since they were last cleaned. Did Henry have something else on his mind for the past couple of months, murder perhaps?

Chapter 23

'Have you found anything yet, Benjamin?' Helen asked.

Benjamin shook his head, a little defeatist at the fact he'd been unable to find anything. She watched him make his way to a large old brown armchair to sit down for a minute. Searching for evidence had been a very demanding process for him, with the fight and being sent into Henry's room to search for evidence. Helen felt bad, she should have been the one to look in Henry's room and let Benjamin examine downstairs, on account of his leg.

'Not yet I'm afraid, Helen, anyway, there's a music box I plan to keep hold of as it looks like it's worth a lot. We could lure Henry back with it, so I'll take it to the station when we're done here. Other than that, I can't find anything that we could use for evidence. Despite what it looks like, I've looked everywhere I can think of,' Benjamin answered apologetically as Helen walked towards another desk-type piece of furniture and pulled open one drawer. 'I've looked in there, Helen,' Benjamin said as she looked at the drawer, puzzling over the fact the drawer on the outside looked as if there were inconsistencies in the diameters of the drawer. Of course, this could be improper craftsmanship, running her hand over and around this piece of furniture, the wood was of good quality. Overall, it was something well made, old age had made it flimsy. But well made. This meant that her initial thought of it being down to poor craftsmanship was wrong. Yes, the dimensions were wrong, but not by fault or age.

Helen proceeded to pull the drawer out of its slot. As she did so, she found you could lift the drawer a little while it was inside its space. Helen was right, the dimensions were wrong, and given they were in their lead suspect's room, this was their lead suspect's paperwork scattered around, he clearly knew something and was now on the run. Helen couldn't help but suspect that the improper proportions were by design.

'The drawers shallower than it should be, Benjamin.' Helen's tone rang with a sense of urgency and excitement as she pulled the drawer out of the socket so fast that she almost fell back with her own force.

Benjamin matched Helen's expression as he heaved himself up and made his way over to her. Only then could Helen see how bad his injuries had become, for Benjamin had forgotten that she was still watching him. Helen saw him make his way over to her, not so much limping on his leg, but dragging it. He didn't need to come to her, she would've come to him.

'When we've done with this, you're going to the hospital,' Helen said sharply as he came alongside her.

'Yes, miss,' he said sarcastically. Helen placed the drawer onto the desk above. Benjamin knocked on a noticeably thinner piece of wood which was sat at the bottom of the drawer about halfway down what Helen reckoned to be the actual size of the drawer. 'It's almost hollow,' Benjamin said, a little surprised at how cleverly Henry had concealed whatever what was inside.

Benjamin's curiosity matched Helen's as they both stood there before Helen pushed back the thin piece of wood. It was so flat, that Helen thought about the possibility of getting a splinter, or it snapping as it was pushed back. There, sat covered in dust, was a passport, green in colour. Some sort of code was punched into the leather in the top corner. The fact that it didn't have the British royal crest but the gold print United States of America, showed that it did not belong to a British citizen, which was odd as Henry was British. This was the proof that they needed that Henry was American.

Thoughts of Henry not being British took over Helen's mind. There were the things she had heard him say that didn't fit with him being British but made sense if Henry was American, along with a document that Helen didn't recognise, but looked official and had the same crest on the top of the document as the passport in her hands.

Passing that on to Benjamin to look at, Helen put everything back in its place, turning her attention once again to the more relevant paperwork and passport Benjamin had in his hand. He was looking over the details, slightly confused at what it all suggested.

'Is this anything of interest, Benjamin? It looks official at any rate,' she said looking at the details on the passport. Same date of birth. Still, for an American national, the man in the picture looked similar to Henry in stature, and there were some aesthetic similarities, but with the name Bertie Newheart, not Henry Boston.

'This doesn't make any sense, why would he have these stashed away?' Benjamin asked himself.

'What is it, Benjamin?' Helen asked again, standing on her tiptoes to see what he was looking at, feeling like a schoolchild who had been left out of something new and exciting.

Lowering his arm slightly to show Helen what it was, he said, 'It's enrolment papers, Helen, but they're American, not British, and not in the correct name, there's no reason for him to have these,' Benjamin explained.

'That's interesting,' Helen said as she and Benjamin compared the passport to the other document. The passport showed the same details as the enrolment papers. Helen worked her way through confirming each detail with Benjamin, looking at him for confirmation as his lip was beginning to get the better of him.

'What if Henry Boston is an alias and his actual name is Bertie Newheart? This proves it, Benjamin, Bertie is who we are really looking for, and this could be in the letter that Mr Hexham pointed out wasn't from him. It was from Henry in his former life as Bertie.'

Just then Benjamin's eyes grew wide. 'We need to leave, Helen. NOW!' Helen threw him a puzzled glance, then she began to smell what had got Benjamin so worried. Smoke, thick smoke coming up from the basement.

They both stood there still as outside people were shouting at the punters to get out. They both watched, frozen for a time, no one knew they were there, and they needed to get out, but how?

As the smoke and flames made their way towards them, under the door and across the floor, shelves caught fire in seconds, paint bubbled in the heat and wood burnt red and black.

Grabbing the evidence and shoving it into his trouser pocket, Benjamin grabbed Helen's hand and ran for the stairs, opening the door only to shut it again as the flames had already engulfed most of the stairs.

Benjamin continued to look for a way out, coughing as the smoke was all around them now, so thick that he could barely see through it to Helen. At the same time, Helen just stood there, not believing that she was about to be burnt alive, and the only thing preventing that from happening was Benjamin. He had already sustained pretty serious injuries. She'd begun to wrap her shawl around the lower part of her face, making sure she didn't breathe in any of the smoke.

Helen's eyes filled up with flames, her blood ran cold as she froze, the smell of smoke alcohol, paper and ink replaced the smell of ladies' perfume.

Before her eyes, the room began to change, she was in Grace's room. The small, well made, complete with hospital corners single bed of Henry's was replaced with a larger more feminine with the lighter coloured sheets of Grace's. Helen couldn't help but hear nothing but the voice of the man who attacked her. 'Don't be stupid, or I'll leave you in the trash.'

Benjamin broke the windowpane and continued to throw the mattress out of the window. Checking where it had landed, he wrapped his arms around Helen as the fire grew more aggressive with the fresh air. Picking her up, Benjamin held her close to him. 'Remember to bend your knees when you hit the floor, Helen, or you'll get hurt, then move off. I'll follow,' he whispered before he threw her out of the broken window.

Helen landed with a thud, without hesitation but with no awareness of what she was doing. Before she knew it, she had rolled off. Benjamin was beginning to jump down, wincing slightly as he landed and rolled off the mattress and onto the street, grabbing Helen as they ran away from the building.

He tugged at Helen to run faster, but there was no chance with Helen still in shock and all but frozen. It was clear that they weren't going to be able to move quickly.

Realising that she was past the point of running for her life, he began to find somewhere they could both stop, until she came round. Finding a shaded area, Benjamin pulled her into it and stood with her as she watched people scatter and fetch pails of water, along with whatever they could to calm the flames. Staff had begun to pull the punters out, still drunk, and unaware of what was happening.

Talking to Helen in a smooth tone and stroking her cheek gently, Benjamin was able to bring Helen round a little. Still holding on to her hand as tightly as he could without crushing her fingers.

'We should head out of town, Helen, just until you can recover, and we'll process what all this means.' He spoke softly, only a little louder than a whisper.

'Yes, Benjamin, that's a good idea,' Helen replied, still unable to close her eyes or move her thoughts away from the fire.

Slowly, they began to pick out the quietest streets and calmest walkways, trying not to draw too much attention to Benjamin's busted lip and injured leg. Helen could still smell the smoke from the building, a fresh waft of it hitting her nose every time her skirt moved around her legs and her eyes burnt every time she blinked as the smoke had taken most of the moisture out.

Still taking the lead, as Helen was in no fit state to be on her own, Benjamin held her arm tightly as he guided her through the streets of drunken men and staff as they scrambled out of the bar always looking around him at all times, every now and again he pulled her closer to him. 'Stay with me, Helen, we're heading to the park,' he whispered to her as he put his arm around her waist. he kept quiet around her as shock had stopped her from taking anything in of what just happened.

'Benjamin, it's all gone, the evidence, it's gone,' Helen said finally.

Sitting her down on a park bench, Benjamin sat down next to her as he handed her the passport and the enrolment papers that he had in his pocket.

'It's not all gone, Helen, here let's look at these again and see what we can piece together.'

Benjamin placed his hand on Helen's as she wrapped her fingers around the evidence. It was as if she didn't want to let them go, for they would disappear.

'You saved them,' Helen said quietly, still in shock but relieved nonetheless, that Benjamin had thought to save the evidence.

Benjamin nodded, then asked, 'You mentioned something about Henry being not who he says he is, Helen, do you remember what you were going to say after that? If we hadn't needed to get out.'

Helen took a moment to try and remember, making faces as she sifted through all the information about the case that was flying around her head along with flames. Placing the two pieces of evidence side by side, she tried to forget about the smell of smoke in her hair and lingering on her clothes.

'Let me think, these are military enrolment papers only given to men serving in the war, correct?' Helen asked, turning to face him. Benjamin nodded again, smiling at her.

'That means this Bertie fellow must have served in the war, this could be tied in with why he's over here as Henry,' Helen said in a moment of clarity. 'But that still doesn't answer anything about where Mary fits into all this.'

'Mary Mortem, Mr Hexham's receptionist?' Benjamin asked, concerned about Helen's actions while his back was turned. Helen remembered he didn't know about every angle she'd been working on in this case.

Chapter 24

Helen paused for a moment, her tunnel vision approach to the case had meant she'd neglected to keep Benjamin informed. She knew she was in trouble, and like a child, didn't want to admit her wrongdoing, but if Helen wanted to get justice for Grace, she needed to tell him. Helen knew that even though Grace was dressed for a night out when Helen had found her, all the evidence she had gathered had said there were other avenues to explore.

'Before you get angry, it was a while ago, and I didn't want you or Detective Arthur stonewalling me over this.' Helen paused before continuing. 'Do you remember the fire in Grace's flat?' Helen asked. Benjamin nodded, looking at her as if to say I don't like where this is going, Helen. 'Right, well before I escaped, I found love letters written to Grace signed with a B.' Helen paused, catching her breath, and steadying her heartbeat as she remembered the bottle bomb, the fire, and her narrow escape. And we now know that Henry and this Mr B are the same, we believe these letters are from Henry back when he went by the name of Bertie' stopping again for a moment. 'I've already cleared Mr Hexham, he's no longer a suspect,' Helen stated as Benjamin took the message from her.

'Why isn't he a suspect anymore?' Benjamin asked, putting the enrolment papers back in his jacket pocket along with the music box.

'Because I went to Mr Hexham, thinking Mr Hexham was Mr B, do you remember?' Benjamin nodded and waited for Helen to continue. 'Well, there were more letters, with the same signature but they were of a less aggressive tone and better written. With better quality paper, they were from Mr Hexham.' Helen paused, watching Benjamin begin to put all this together. 'As you remember me telling you he'd told me that they had broken the affair off and then there's the letter to Grace saying he was happy to admire her from a distance. He also grieves too much for a guilty party.' After a moment of silence, Helen couldn't hold her excitement in any longer.

'Don't you see Bertie's American? Possibly related to the war, he's over here as Henry, and the letter, addressed to Grace. They must have some romantic connection that needed to end for Bertie to become Henry.' Helen paused giving Benjamin a chance to catch up.

'Helen, it sounds good but if Bertie's American and Grace English, how did they meet and why did you keep this from me?'

Benjamin questioned Helen, for he had grown familiar with Helen's way of thinking through a problem, looking into every piece of evidence she could get with a fine-tooth comb, and she wouldn't pull a theory out of nowhere. Still, he couldn't follow where her approach had come from.

'Helen, are you sure this all links together? It's definitely interesting and a good lead, but it's all conjecture. For all you know, Mr Hexham is the killer and wrote different letters to throw you off course. If you'd come to me with this earlier, I could have told you this and saved you time,' Benjamin said, as concern filled his words.

'I'm sorry, Benjamin, I wanted to, but I just haven't found

the time to other than now,' Helen stated apologetically. Benjamin had a point; she knew where to find him. After listening to Helen's apology, Benjamin sighed.

'You still need evidence that is solid, we can't build a case on circumstance,' Benjamin finally said, poking fun at Helen's excitement.

'You're the police, Deputy James, you figure it out,' Helen joked, as a smile broke over her face. Benjamin's face mimicked hers.

'You're beautiful when you smile, Helen,' Benjamin said looking up from the evidence in his hands. Catching Helen unaware, he placed his lips on hers and closed them, staying there for a moment as Helen tightened her grip.

Once again it was time for them to go home. She took Benjamin's arm.

'You promise me you'll get yourself seen to, Benjamin, you can't very well catch Bertie if you're nursing those injuries.'

'Yes, Helen, I'll go to the station and get myself seen to by the pathologist if that makes you feel better,' Benjamin said, the pain from his injuries showing itself once again. Helen reckoned that his adrenaline had now subsided.

'Yes, Benjamin, it would make me feel much better,' Helen answered, once again disappearing into her own mind. Where did Bertie and Grace meet and how does this tie in with Bertie being the killer?

After having one of the most restful night's sleep, she'd had in a while, Helen woke to feel oddly light in her step. As the morning sun shone its wintery warmth through the thin pane of glass into her room, her mind whirled with pictures of Benjamin and his busted-up lip. The fact that her being in peril was the reason behind his busted-up mouth didn't seem to factor in her mind at all as she pinned her hair up while dust glistened like glitter as it twisted and fell to the floor. Helen found herself almost dancing around her room as she got ready for work.

Even the Ellentons looked just as perplexed as the other staff members at this new gait she was carrying.

'Are you okay, Helen?' Mrs Ellenton asked, gauging Helen's step and was clearly surmising what had happened to Helen. It wasn't long ago that she walked as if she was floating along the delicate sky.

'Yes, miss, I'm perfectly fine, miss, just had a long-needed restful sleep,' Helen replied, reminding herself that she was being watched, if she wanted to keep her personal and professional life separate, she wasn't to allow herself to be distracted by what was going on between her and Benjamin. Mrs Ellenton gave Helen an all-knowing look, making Helen have to hide behind a serving plate while serving the children their meal in order not to allow anyone to see her blush red.

Helen went about the rest of her day as best she could. Just like any other day, finding herself smiling like a silly schoolchild whenever she didn't have something else to occupy her mind. Luckily for Helen, there was plenty to do as the Ellentons had been hosting a dinner, and one of their guests had drunk too much to go home safely.

As Helen assisted Dolly in cleaning and making ready one of the many spare rooms that were required that evening, Helen's sleeve rolled up, showing some slight bruising from the ropes she'd had been bound in the night before. Realising this, Helen's eyes widened as she shoved her sleeves back over the bruises so hard that for a moment her skin throbbed with the pain of the sensitive skin having been touched. She hoped the other maid hadn't noticed. Looking at her, Helen couldn't decipher if she had.

As the evening fell, Helen found herself desperate for a distraction, helping the house cleaners with needlework, dishes, lighting fires, anything to keep her mind off the case. More importantly off Benjamin. Pinching herself whenever her mind wandered over the investigation and to him, she reminded herself that a roof over her head was more important than a silly little infatuation with a young man. She couldn't afford to lose her job.

Once the day came to an end, and she thought she had succeeded in her endeavour not to let Benjamin into this part of her life, Dolly came up to her and said, 'There's a police officer in the courtyard asking for you, miss. He says you'll know what it's about?'

Helen ignored Dolly's attempt at fishing for some gossip as she dried her hands on a cloth and told the maid to continue with her duties as she walked towards where Benjamin would be waiting for her.

Helen noticed that he was in his uniform and that the courtyard was heaving with staff. 'Deputy James, how may I help you?'

He waited for Helen to get a little closer, as he needed to speak to her without causing gossip, then Benjamin said, slightly hushed. 'I've been in contact with the American embassy to see what information they can give us on this Bertie character. I can't discuss it here, could you meet me in the library later and I'll give you the details then?' Benjamin stood up straight and shot a disapproving glance at the maid who had taken a little too long folding a linen sheet, ready to be brought inside.

Chapter 25

Helen nodded and left to catch up with Dolly. Based on what Benjamin had said, Helen knew that her theory about Henry being Bertie from America was correct. Helen knew then that there was a sizeable chunk of the timeline she was still missing. They would need to find out who Henry was as Bertie, where he came from, and why was he here as Henry. Helen hoped this was the information Benjamin had that she would find out at the library later. She needed to process all of this, but after reminding the maid of her place. A twinge of embarrassment filled Helen, but she remembered that as far as the maid could see they were talking professionally, Benjamin was in his uniform and so was she.

'You know not to eavesdrop, Dolly. You understand I was talking to the Deputy about something private, don't you? If you heard anything I expect you to keep it to yourself, are we clear?' Helen said, disciplining the maid.

'Yes, miss, I heard nothing,' Dolly replied as she looked down at the sheets that were folded and placed them in a large basket.

After climbing the stairs to her room with a little more ease than she had done for a while, Helen made for her desk. Lowering herself in her chair slowly for the bruises had not yet left her, she pulled out a blank piece of paper, something to write with and the notes she had taken. Head bowing as her hand lifted, she was ready to take notes.

After writing for so long and holding her pen so hard that her hand ached as her muscles shook with the effort, she stopped to look at what she had written. After reading it over again multiple times she stared in disbelief at what she had written.

There were next to no facts, or anything to do with the case. It was all Benjamin, how he thought quickly enough to get her out of the fire. The fight he had with who they now know was Bertie. Rolling her eyes in despair, she placed her head in her hands and cried for it all to end. How many times would she nearly have to die for them to solve the case? Helen continued to sob until her cheeks were red raw, and her ribs jabbed at her. Looking at her hands, pools of tears covered both of them slowly dripping back onto her desk.

Helen reminded herself she had duties to fulfil. Wiping her hands on her apron, she headed out of her room using the washbasin, splashing her face with some cold water. The quicker Helen could solve it, the faster she could return to normal.

She strolled through the marketplace, giving and receiving nods from the stall owners and pondering what Benjamin had said.

'He's slipped up once, he'll slip up again.' Helen couldn't help but feel uneasy at his logic, sure he could now be panicking about getting caught. But that was a reaction Mary would take, to Helen it felt more likely Bertie would go underground. Shuddering at what that would do to Benjamin's reputation, Helen's body shivered. Had she pushed Benjamin into making an unwise career move? This didn't last long as Helen reminded herself that Benjamin was a grown man, able to make his own choices in life. Still, she couldn't shake the guilt completely, he was doing this for her.

Helen finished up her last purchase of the day. Turning around, she spotted a familiar-looking face from across the crowd. Helen couldn't quite tell if it was who she thought it was, there were too many people in the way. Shifting slightly Helen saw it was who she thought it was, they were standing right there, and they hadn't noticed Helen yet.

Helen couldn't believe her luck, the only person that hadn't run away or was dead, and who could confirm any of Benjamin's theory was just out of reach of her.

As all the visions came flooding back to Helen regarding what the person had been complicit in, Helen tried to keep herself from losing her temper at them.

Helen reminded herself that she wasn't really in a fit state to start going through town, but there wasn't any chance that they would meet. Helen watched as she tried to figure out what they were doing, there was also that this was another trap set out for Helen and she didn't have Benjamin to prevent her from coming to harm. Helen couldn't help herself, she had to get their attention.

'Mary!' Helen shouted, pushing her way through the crowds towards her. Helen refused to let her target disappear from view before she had a chance to speak to her.

Dodging between people, stalls and the odd stray dog, Helen was adamant not to let Mary get away, something about the mix of anger at Mary for putting Helen in danger and seemingly turning a blind eye to what Bertie had done to her work colleague.

As her side was still a little sore from being beaten, Helen couldn't deny the little tinkering of revenge. If she could catch Mary and make her confess to having a hand in Helen's kidnapping then, Benjamin would be able to question her about Grace's murder. But Helen had to catch her first.

Mary spun around as her eyes grew wide at seeing Helen briskly making her way through the square towards her. As her eyes widened even more, her hand flew up to her face. Mary had seen Helen watching her. After a brief second of disbelief, Mary took off. Helen began to call the onlookers to move out of her way. Pushing the handles of the basket further up her shoulder she began to chase Mary from the market and out on to the streets surrounding it. Not once did Helen allow Mary to escape her sight.

'Go away,' Mary shouted back, beginning to panic at how close Helen was. People started to mutter and stare at the two women playing a high stakes game of cat and mouse.

Helen desperately tried to match Mary's pace as they both weaved in and out of the sea of people. There were mothers desperately trying to move their children out of the way and sobering up folk only just managing to move out of the way of Mary. Still, in the process, moving directly into Helen's path. Every muscle in Helen's body screamed, but Helen could not let Mary go.

Finally grabbing Mary's wrist. 'You said you knew something about Grace, Mary, what was it?' Helen's tone was desperate. All of the case she had worked so hard for and risked her life for hinged on Mary telling her the truth.

'Go away,' Mary shouted, trying to wriggle her wrist free from Helen's grasp, but years of lifting and other such domestic jobs had taught Helen how to keep a good grip.

'Tell me what you were going to say, Mary, for the love of Grace, she was your friend.' Helen's final plea for information backfired as Mary suddenly stopped wriggling.

'I am no friend of Grace's, she was going to ruin

everything,' Mary blurted out before running at full speed out of the market.

Helen couldn't get what the 'everything' was that Mary was talking about. Options whirled around Helen's head. Could it have been related to Grace's job, however thin? Helen hoped that it was a case of Bertie taking advantage of Mary's jealousy over Grace. That left a personal source of motivation, but what would that be. All this occupied Helen's mind as she travelled to the library to meet Benjamin, her body throbbing, and her eyes closing slowly after her chase with Mary.

Chapter 26

She stopped at the bottom of the stairs of the library, watching the clouds in the sky grow dark and begin to rain down on the pavement below. Sucking all the warmth out of the air, her place of sanctuary had been torn from her, instead, it was just another grey building on a street of grey buildings. What once had offered her an escape from reality now forced her to face it head-on.

Climbing up the stairs and into the foyer, she could smell the tobacco again and the hushed chatter of the gentlemen, the librarian checking in books and hushed noises of the school children. This time, instead of the sounds being part of the journey of escaping, they felt cold. Immediately after she opened the door, her chest tightened. She reacted to the burning pain of her body, reminding herself that she would not be in this much pain if Helen hadn't fallen for Mary's and Bertie's trap a few days before. Her eyes darted from left to right, taking everyone in, looking for anything suspicious. Helen headed to her usual chair. Helen could see the street, so she could wait for Benjamin's arrival. Helen made her way towards the chair she had begun this journey from, knowing that even though the rest of the library felt cold, the chair would still be there ready to provide her with some solace.

Turning the corner, feeling the stone cooling in the afternoon sun, she saw Benjamin reading the newspaper article about the fire a couple of days before. Helen fought back images of the flames, making quick work of the bar, helped along by the masses of accelerants in the building.

'Benjamin, did you get anything from the American embassy?' Helen whispered, attracting his attention. Benjamin shot up and led her round to the chair facing him.

Helen sank into the armchair. Although this wasn't the chair she'd had in mind, this one held her upright more while not pressing up against her too much, allowing her to mask the pain she was in from Benjamin. That would no doubt lead to her having to admit she'd chased Mary through town, which Helen knew would make him not best pleased with her. Had it been a second kidnapping attempt or even silencing, Helen would have fallen for it hook, line and sinker.

'Yes, Helen, I believe I may have found something to change your theory into fact,' Benjamin began, pausing only to gauge Helen's reaction, to see whether Helen had recovered enough to be told about what he had found out from the American embassy. 'I contacted the American embassy last night after what had happened and the evidence we found, to see if they had any record of a Bertie Newheart.'

'Go on, Benjamin.' Helen's eagerness to prove her theory was clear in her tone and she struggled to keep herself from coming to his side to see what he had discovered.

'They did have a soldier by that name stationed in Devon who was supposed to go to the Somme, but he deserted a few days before.'

'So, he's a deserter from the American army, that gives him the skill to kill and evade the police, but it doesn't give us the reason why Mary fits into all this,' Helen mused aloud as she sat back in the leather chair.

'I have a theory on what may have been the motivation on Bertie's part, Helen.' Benjamin put forward, pausing as Helen turned her head to face him as she had begun to gaze out the window, lost in thought. 'Grace's hometown is in Devon, I dug into Grace's record as well as this Bertie character. What if they knew each other from while he was stationed there, as the letter suggests? If he is the 'B' in the message, they were stepping out, and Grace could've blown his cover, the punishment for deserting is a court martial for enlisted members and sometimes they are shot, Helen. Bertie could have killed Grace to keep his cover story intact.'

Helen pondered the theory for a moment then spoke. 'It's plausible, Benjamin, but how could Bertie know that Grace would inform the police? If she loved him, wouldn't she keep his secret if she knew. There are still a lot of variables.'

'In my experience, that means we're getting close to the facts of the matter, Helen. Remember, we are all human and have ever-changing motivations,' Benjamin replied softly watching Helen once again disappear into her thoughts for he had grown to love her doing so.

After a while of quiet deliberation, Helen could feel Benjamin's warm hand on hers, jumping slightly as she spun her head round to look at him, smiling gently at her. 'I need to leave now, Helen, would you like me to walk you home, or will you be okay going home on your own.'

'No, Benjamin, you head off, I could do with some time to think further on all this,' Helen replied, feeling her bruises reject the idea of moving. She had sat down too long to move quickly, and she didn't want him to see her like that.

Benjamin nodded, then kissed the back of her hand gently and said, 'Look after yourself, Helen.' Then disappeared around the corner and out onto the street.

Watching Benjamin as he passed the window, striding towards the station, Helen began to reflect on what he'd said, this time in more detail, taking advantage of the rest away from him and anybody else who would notice her in pain to ease her ribs and side.

Benjamin's new information about Bertie and Grace being in Devon at the same time put them together, geographically at least. Helen puzzled as she moved past the bread stall on her way home. Pausing for a moment to take in the smell of fresh bread cooking in the large ovens, try as she might, she couldn't help but turn to face the window and watch as the baker began preparing the dough.

The rhythmic movement of his hands as he hit the dough, then rolling it into shapes ready for the oven. Then as if keeping herself on track the question about Bertie and Grace offered itself up again. If they were together that gave them a connection but how does that equate to one of them murdering the other five years later? Helen could not get past that as things stood in the case, Bertie had killed Grace out of the blue. However, Benjamin was right; we all have continually changed motivations for taking specific actions. This did not feel to Helen like a random act, poison required skill, planning and faultless execution. Helen knew that something must have gone wrong five years ago to warrant Bertie having the need to kill Grace.

Chapter 27

Waking up before dawn, Helen busied herself with the chores, giving herself as much time as possible to go to Mr Hexham to enquire about Mary and her connection to Grace. There was no apparent link between them which annoyed her, there must be a reason for Mary to either turn a blind eye to what was happening between Grace and Bertie or be an accomplice.

Even if she was an accomplice, she still needed the motive to get involved. Helen knew Mary wouldn't be at work today but wondered where she had gone, The Locus Nectar had burnt down, and she had to be careful. The police wanted her, and she also knew Helen was involved in solving Grace's murder.

Helen excused herself after morning briefing and headed out to town, taking a ride in one of the delivery vans as far into town as possible. Helen could still get jobs done while she was in town after she was done asking Mr Hexham questions.

Entering the solicitor's and closing the door behind her, she barely had time to breathe before Mr Hexham had popped his head around the office door.

'Come in, Helen.' He sounded worse than the last time she had heard him speak.

There was no sound of anything as Helen made her way through to Mr Hexham's office. Despite the warm tones of the paint covering the walls, the office felt cold.

'I'm so sorry to bring this back up, Mr Hexham,' Helen

started as she settled herself down in the chair, finding the most comfortable place to sit while having sore ribs. 'But I need to know some details about Grace, and to know where another one of your workers is if you know at all.' Helen placed a hand on his arm. As she gently squeezed, all she could feel under his suit was skin and bone, his frailty clear, grief had taken his appetite. He was working himself to the grave. He nodded.

'What is it you want to know about Grace, Helen?' Mr Hexham asked, tired and worn with grief.

'How long has Grace lived here, Mr Hexham? Has she mentioned this at all to you?' Helen asked as delicately as she could. Mr Hexham sighed.

'Grace had only been here for five to six months before she died. She mentioned living in Devon before moving here. Grace was optimistic about living in a city up to a couple of weeks before her death. That's when she called it off with me and said moving was all a mistake,' Mr Hexham said, his eyes shutting slowly as painful memories filled his head, shoulders rolling forward and in as if he was sinking into himself.

Helen decided to ask about Mary.

'I need to talk to Mary, Mr Hexham, do you know where she is?' Helen spoke softly. Mr Hexham just shook his head, and waves of grief came over him once more.

'Thank you, Mr Hexham, that's really helpful, I think I can begin to put the pieces together now, and that's down to you,' Helen said, as she left for somewhere she could find some peace and quiet to put everything into place.

Finding herself in the park, her mind whirled, extending her timeline in her mind ready to add it to the hard copy she had in her room at the Ellentons' and the series of events leading to Grace's death.

Helen ran through all she knew about Bertie before he

became Henry, charting the reason Bertie felt the need to change his name and travel under an alias. Bertie was an American soldier posted in Devon where Grace lived at the same time. Then he begins pursuing a relationship with Helen's victim, Grace.

Helen could see the allure of dating such a man, a good-looking American soldier who could be called away any day to go and fight. For a young woman, the adventure and excitement would be hard to resist.

Bertie is then faced with this genuine reality as he's ordered to go back to his station, then from there go to France to fight at the Somme. Thinking, however wrongly, that deserting was a better idea, Bertie realises that for this plan to work, he would have to end things with Grace.

Writing the letter that Helen was given by Mr Hexham signed 'B' he does just that, then travels here, to Nottingham. Under the alias Henry Boston.

In his new life as Henry, he builds a company, the Locus Nectar, and starts some sort of connection with Mary. Then Grace appears. She knows who he really is, and now he's being faced with being discovered, the only way to guarantee her silence is to kill her, using Mary as the diversion or accomplice. At any rate, Helen had her killer in her sights.

'It's time to catch the mouse,' Helen whispered as she beckoned a street boy to send a note with a time, location, and date to Benjamin, for she would need his help to catch Henry.

Watching the young street boy, Helen couldn't help but try to imagine Benjamin as a young boy taking such errands eager to have a bit of coin in their pocket. As the street boy faded into the distance, Helen made her way home, she had chores to finish. Helen needed to organise her leave to be able to meet Benjamin at the time she had allocated to catch the killer. She will solve her case.

Waiting in the park the following afternoon, Helen's mind ran wild with the facts of the case. The only thing was how to make it all viable enough to actually pursue Henry, or rather Bertie.

'Helen,' Benjamin called as he picked up his pace to come and sit next to her on the bench. 'You've found something, haven't you? What have you found?' He sounded just as excited as Helen was feeling.

'Yes, Benjamin, I have, but it's only speculation, it doesn't have all that much evidence to prove my theory. I think you'll have to prove it when you catch Henry, aka, Bertie, I think that I've found something out that backs your theory about Bertie and Grace stepping out while he was stationed in Devon.'

Benjamin looked puzzled, 'Helen, what information? I know I theorised on them stepping out, but you seem very sure that they did, where is your evidence?'

Helen continued, explaining her hypothesis, beginning from when Benjamin thought about them stepping out as a motive for murder. Helen explained that Mr Hexham had placed Grace in Devon at the same time.

'Then there's that random letter from a Mr B who I believe to be Bertie that matches the timescale for Grace moving to Nottingham and her subsequent death. We've got everything we need: means, motive and a timeline for when all this happened,' she explained, her excitement increasing with every fact.

Helen stopped, taking in Benjamin's reaction. He was beginning to put things together in his own mind. 'But why kill her, that would mean there's a five-year gap between

Bertie deserting, breaking things off with Grace and killing her.' Benjamin used his hands like a weighing scale moving them up and down as if weighing his options.

Helen sighed. 'Bertie is under an assumed name hiding from the law, if Grace is still hurt at him dumping her, and recognises him, then she could blow the whistle and have him arrested for desertion. A good motive to kill someone, don't you think?' Helen gave him a sidewards glance, he'd placed the missing piece of the puzzle together.

Sighing, Benjamin spoke. 'I don't suppose you're going to leave this alone, and in my hands to draw him out, are you?' he asked, somehow knowing that it wasn't likely, but Helen's reaction made him laugh all the same.

'Absolutely not. I saw this case began; I want to finish it.' Helen's rebellious streak came out once again.

'All right then, I think I have a plan,' Benjamin said with a smile. Turning to face her, he revealed his plan.

'Thank you for letting me finish this, Benjamin,' Helen said as he dropped her off at the Ellentons.'

'Did I really have a choice?' Benjamin asked rhetorically.

Helen laughed as she answered. 'No, I don't think you did.' He nodded before she turned to walk away.

Somehow, Helen's heart sank a little as she stepped away from him. Would she see as much of Benjamin without having a case to solve or a perpetrator to chase? Was all of this between her and Benjamin so entangled with the investigation that it would die if there wasn't an inquiry to be had? A case to be solved?

Opening the servants' entrance door, Helen set about completing the tasks she had set out to do that evening, Benjamin, the case, and the failed attempt at an arrest of their suspect was near to her mind, they still had a plan to find him. Still, Helen couldn't shake the feeling that he had only thought of the most straightforward action to solve the case. If Bertie was going to avoid the police after committing murder, then nearly getting arrested, surely that would mean going to an auction with a high police presence would be the last thing on his mind. Bertie was smarter than that. With that in mind, she set about getting ready for the next day followed by bed. Tomorrow would be a big day. The day they try and catch Bertie.

Waking up early with a new sense of purpose, Helen made quick work of the morning briefing and her chores, she didn't want to miss catching Bertie. Helen knew Benjamin had roped Detective Arthur into being there. Possibly even promised him the collar. Helen's heart stopped. What was Benjamin trying to do, Helen understood that Detective Arthur was the senior police officer and Benjamin's superior. Helen knew she can't arrest Bertie as she's a civilian. Still, Detective Arthur had all but given up on Grace. Why would he be the one to capture Bertie? Police procedure meant that the officer who handled the case, which was Benjamin, had the collar. Helen worried that she'd caused trouble between them. Helen hated that thought. She had never set out to create a problem between them. However, she couldn't think of any other reason for Deputy James to allow Detective Arthur to be involved in the arrest of a man that if the Detective had anything to say about it, would have gone free.

Benjamin planned to 'auction off' the music box, it had been made of ivory so a thing of value. Benjamin hoped that, if Bertie hadn't already skipped the country there was a possibility there was some chance that if the box has enough value for Bertie, then he may appear to regain possession of it.

Helen thought his plan a little concerning; there was no guarantee that Bertie was still in the country. What makes Benjamin think Bertie has enough sentimentality for the box, to risk capture?

As Helen stood on the outskirts of the fake auction, she took in the crowd of undercover police officers and eager buyers, having no idea that this was a sting. She's charged with spotting and following Bertie if he should show.

The auction had got off to a good start, it had a few other non-case related items he had put up for sale first. A few, Helen was almost tempted to bid for herself. Still, she refrained as she needed to keep her focus on looking for Bertie. Scanning the crowd, she could recognise the two junior officers, and there was Benjamin making his rounds of the group occasionally stopping to talk to someone, the other undercover police Helen presumed.

The item that Benjamin had planned to use as bait for Bertie had come up for sale. Helen watched as each officer, in turn, shuffled slightly ready to pounce on Bertie once he'd given away where he was. Helen continued to scan the crowd. As planned, one of the officers pretended to buy it, for it needed to be kept for evidence. The item was a dark wooden jewellery box which had been found in a safe with an ivory lid. A beautiful box, Helen mused, as the auction went on with the other items of the day. Every officer, and Helen, were a little deflated at the failed sting.

'Have you spotted him yet, Helen?' Benjamin asked once the auction was in full swing.

'No, Benjamin, I haven't,' Helen replied, a little frustrated at the apparent failure of the sting.

'We'll get him, Helen.' Benjamin sought to soothe her

frustration. 'Perhaps not today but we will get him.'

Helen sighed as Benjamin indicated to stop for the day. 'I've been in contact with the police at Dover. I've sent across a picture of Bertie as himself and of his alias, Henry, with the information that he's wanted in connection with deserting the war effort and the murder, Helen.' Looking down at her, putting his hands on hers, meeting her gaze, he carried on. 'If he is trying to skip the country, odds are he'll flee to France now the war is over. If he does, they'll arrest him and bring him to us,' Benjamin said trying to cheer her up. 'He will be caught, Helen, perhaps not today but soon, he knows he can't stay long, so he will have to do a runner soon.'

Not feeling very comforted, Helen appreciated what Benjamin was saying. He was right. 'Thank you for the gesture, Benjamin, but it doesn't change the fact he's out there, which means I've not completed my moral duty to give Grace justice. Bertie is still roaming free.'

Benjamin nodded, for what Helen was saying was true. Bertie was still a free man, on the run, but free all the same.

Chapter 28

'That reminds me, Helen, we will need your notes on the investigation and any evidence you've collected, it'll help us put Bertie away when we catch him. Otherwise, it's all speculation, and we would have to drop the whole thing, and then Bertie really will be a free man.'

Helen's back straightened, she had worked so hard on making sure Grace got her justice, often risking her own life. Now Benjamin, of all people, wanted the fruits of her labour. Helen looked at him. He realised Helen wasn't keen on giving up her notes and subsequently all her hard work to the police. To Detective Arthur, who at every step of this investigation that he knew about had sought to diminish her efforts and then when that didn't work, attempted to close her out of the case altogether.

'I know it's a big ask after you have worked so hard, but the evidence I've seen from you is good, and you've done more than me, and Detective Arthur could have done to find Bertie. Now, let me make sure he goes away for what he's done.' Benjamin pleaded with her.

'All right, Benjamin, I suppose you're right, I'll give you my notes and the evidence that I have.' Helen took in Benjamin's relief that she had not kicked up about having to hand over her work without so much as a thank you.

'Thank you, Helen, it could also help us figure out where

he might head to if he is trying to get out of town,' Benjamin said in an attempt to be sensitive to Helen's investment in the case.

'I understand, Benjamin, but please don't let Detective Arthur take all the credit for my work, I don't want the praise, but neither do I want him to take it.' Helen could hear how confused she sounded. Who would then take the credit for Bertie's apprehension, but somehow Benjamin seemed to know where she was coming from and understood what she wanted.

'Do you want me to suggest to Detective Arthur to let me take this arrest and say we had some outside help; would that suit you?' Benjamin explained that if Detective Arthur took the arrest, then he would be there when Detective Arthur would have to answer to the press about how he'd found the killer. Something that would not go down well for him, for Detective Arthur would have to admit that he had help from outside the police force. Also, if he had the arrest, it would mean that Detective Arthur would then need to do the paperwork, something else he knew Detective Arthur wasn't fond of doing.

Helen's shoulders relaxed as the tension and the defensiveness left her, for, through her babbling, he understood what she had said enough to be able to find her desired solution. 'Yes, Benjamin, something like that. I can't afford to have the Ellentons think I'm not responsible. As far as they're aware I've just been answering questions and helping you and Detective Arthur with your inquiries.' Helen's eyes widened at the fact that she had unwittily lied to them, something she did not typically make a habit of.

Benjamin nodded his head 'Okay, Helen, I'll try and keep

the fact that you did most of the work here quiet. But promise me you'll try and keep your head down for a little while longer. I don't want Bertie trying to find you while we're on this wild goose chase to find him.'

It was Helen's turn to nod her head. 'Yes, Benjamin, I think that's enough case solving for me for a little while.'

Helen watched as he walked away to go and regroup with the rest of the police officers he had commissioned to operate the sting.

Breathing slowly, she turned away from the square. As she did so she couldn't help but feel as if the case wasn't quite finished, for one they hadn't caught Bertie yet. As Benjamin suggested, unless Bertie was put away behind bars, Helen wasn't safe, not really, and finally, they would still need to find Mary.

Walking back through town, Helen felt both angry and upset at the fact that their efforts today had failed to catch Bertie. It suggested that he had fled either just the city or the country altogether. Could it be that it was too late? The time for them to catch him had run out, would Grace's murder remain an open case, forever?

Entering her room at the Ellentons' house, she looked at its bare walls and plain sheets, this case had been the most exciting thing she had done for a while. Now she was to go back to normal, Helen wasn't even sure she knew what an average day was any more. For all Helen wasn't a fan of being kidnapped, and tied up, neither did she like the idea that Bertie, having failed to get Helen through other means, would go back to what he knew and try to drug her. Helen had seen into a side of the world that intrigued her and that she needed to learn more about.

Being conscious of not getting too tied up in what she was missing, she organised her desk, collating all her notes. Pulling the letters out from the drawer where Helen had kept them, the weight of them struck her, never had she lifted all her notes on the investigation altogether at the same time.

Separating the notes from the Grace Andrews case and any records relating to her attack and her kidnapping, Helen put it all into her satchel.

Helen couldn't help but smile, for judging by the weight alone, whoever it was that would help Bertie in court try and plead his innocence, if that was what he planned, would have one hell of a job on his hands.

Holding the notes in her hands for a moment, Helen knew all this work could still amount to nothing. Bertie could avoid capture and get away with what he had done to Grace, and if he was involved in any way with Helen's attack at the market, which seemed ever more likely, they could get Bertie for that, at least, and he could still be punished for his crimes.

Looking down at her notes, was she ready to hand all her work over just like that? Helen didn't want recognition from the public. Still, some sort of acknowledgement from Detective Arthur would have been what she was going for. Helen wanted him to admit he was wrong about her and should not have dismissed her so coldly.

Placing the bag on her chair and her notes carefully in the bag, Helen made her way down into the kitchen, and out into the main house to carry on with the tasks of the day. She would give Benjamin her notes later as she expected he would be busy with the paperwork of closing the case for good.

With the sun streaming down through her window, Helen made ready for the day, she would be present for morning briefing then she would excuse herself and go into town with her notes and hand them over when there was space in her day to do so. Helen could also ask Benjamin if he wanted to go out for an evening stroll after work with her, though she had no idea what they would talk about now.

Helen couldn't help but worry that there wasn't anything to talk to each other about anymore, but there must be something they could talk about that wasn't case related, they didn't know each other all that well already, did they?

Putting that out of her mind as she grabbed the bag with the notes in it, Helen made for the station, past the people bustling by and narrowly missing a horse and cart, the weight of the bag whacking her side every time she took a step.

Helen noted that for all its weight, it only weighed about a half of Grace's weight. She could still move about quite quickly. Impressed at herself, Helen turned off the street and trotted up the police station stairs.

Standing in the reception area, Helen noted everything looked quite calm compared to what she had expected. Looking through some of the office doorways that had been kept ajar, Helen could see Benjamin in his office, tiny compared to Detective Arthur's. Still, somehow it felt warmer, she could see Benjamin sat at his desk with a pen in his hand, a concentrated look on his face.

She knocked on the door frame lightly. 'Come in.' Benjamin spoke clearly still very distracted by the paperwork on his desk. Helen couldn't help but smile.

'I've got some more paperwork for you, Deputy James.' Helen had to suppress a laugh at the look on his face as he finished writing his sentence before looking up and realised it was her with the notes he'd asked for.

'The face you had on just now, do you not like paperwork?' she joked, opening up her bag on a space he had made for it.

'Not when it takes so long, Helen, no I don't,' he replied, very much, not joking.

Helen apologised and said, 'Here is all that I have on the Grace Andrews' case, I hope this helps.' Benjamin nodded, eyeing up the pile that had erupted on his desk. 'Are you going to be free this evening?' Helen asked, thinking the answer would be a no.

'It'll be late if at all, Helen, to be honest. It looks like I'm in for a long night, until this is all filed,' Benjamin replied indicating at the files and loose bits of paper on his desk. 'Another time, perhaps?' he asked as he sat back in his chair. Helen nodded and returned home to finish up what needed to be done.

Chapter 29

A few weeks passed; all was quiet. Newspapers stopped reporting on Grace's murder. Benjamin hadn't called on Helen about her offer to go out for a drink, or about the case. Wanted posters appeared on lampposts. Each pamphlet contained Mary's picture and a picture of Bertie. Some had a picture of him as his alias, Henry.

Helen knew that Deputy James now had to take the lead, as Helen was limited as to what she could do to tidy all the strands of the case together. The ball was in Deputy James's court now. The only way that would change would be if Helen saw either Mary or Bertie, and report back to Benjamin, where it was she had seen them. With Bertie having already escaped once and Mary not having been seen for weeks, Helen didn't fancy her chances of that happening. Both Bertie and Mary knew the police would still chase any leads about their whereabouts, so they would need to keep their heads low to avoid capture.

Helen went about assisting some new maids that had been hired with some rudimentary chores, for she wanted to show them how she expected them to fulfil their tasks. As she did so, Helen began wondering how the investigation had ended and whether her notes on the case, had in fact, been helpful.

Helen made plans to see Benjamin in her lunch break to see if the case had gone to court. Or whether they were still looking for Bertie and Mary. Somehow Helen felt she hadn't completed her task until both Mary and Bertie were caught and brought to trial. Watching the clock tick by, it was time for Helen to leave for the station.

Making her way through town, Helen thought about how she could get the information she needed out of Benjamin. It had been a significant risk to let Helen into the investigation in the first place, given it was technically against protocol. It could have led to the entire case never making it to court at all.

Helen knew that this could overstep the mark yet again, but she couldn't stand having a task half done, a goal only partially achieved. The two murder suspects in her case, were still missing. On the loose, free to kill again, Justice had not yet been served.

Once in the station, Helen looked around for Benjamin. Locking eyes with a police officer behind the reception desk, she asked if she could see him.

'Deputy James is downstairs doing interviews, wait in his office, and I'll let him know you're here,' he called with a gruff tone to his voice. Helen nodded and made her way across the foyer and into Deputy James' office.

As Helen sat waiting, she noticed the case file on Grace Andrews's murder was on his desk. Dead centre with nothing else around it. Helen looked at it for what seemed to be forever, wondering if she should take a look inside for a moment. The information Helen had come for was in there all along. Helen wouldn't have to disturb Benjamin. She could be there and gone before he was done interviewing downstairs.

Helen began to reach for the file as Benjamin walked in at quite a fast pace.

'Sorry to keep you waiting, Helen, what do you need?'

Benjamin asked as he sat down with a sigh. Helen began to answer.

'I just wanted to know if you've found either of our suspects yet?' Helen answered.

Benjamin smiled. 'I thought you'd said that was enough mystery solving for you.'

Helen chuckled, then replied, 'I thought you were going to find them quicker than this.' She was joking at how they'd not been able to find either of them, Benjamin laughed back, then spoke.

'I think I might have a way of luring them out, it's been a while since the auction so they could have a false sense of security by now.' Benjamin spoke softly as if musing over his plan.

'Are you going to plan another sting, Benjamin?' Helen asked, sounding a little too eager for that to be true.

'No, Helen, not quite. As you know there are wanted pamphlets all over town showing our suspects' faces, with an award attached for any actionable information or a sighting,' Benjamin explained as Helen listened closely, waiting for his plan to be revealed. 'A little street kid had come up to me the other week. He'd said that he'd seen a couple come in and out of one of the old factories just outside of town. The gentleman matches the picture, but the lady always looks down and so he couldn't see her face.'

'So, what's your plan, Benjamin?' Helen asked. 'Have you verified the information before you go round knocking on doors?' Helen couldn't help but think that the street boy might have just said what the police officers wanted to hear to get the reward money.

'Yes, I've sent out one of our rookies to watch the factory

undercover. The boy's information is right, we just need to catch them. I really don't want to have to raid the factory. That's their territory, so the chances of escape are high. We need a way to get them while they're out in the open.' Benjamin continued rocking his chair on one leg. 'My plan is to have them followed so that we can, on a day-by-day basis, see what their routines are. That way we know where they are and when the best time to make an arrest would be.' Helen couldn't help but think that his plan wasn't likely to work, after all Bertie was a former soldier and would notice if someone was following them. There's the fact that they may know better than to follow a predictable routine.

Once again, Helen's facial expressions had betrayed her thoughts to Benjamin. 'You don't think it'll work, do you, Helen?' Benjamin asked, but his tone remained light-hearted.

'I can't help but think that you're underestimating Bertie, Benjamin. Your plan may work if we were to catch someone inexperienced in avoiding the police. Still, Bertie has managed to avoid being discovered not just by the police, but also by the military. It's a good starting point for a plan, it just needs work.'

Benjamin nodded, for he could see where Helen was going in her thoughts. 'Do you have another plan, Helen?' he asked.

'Not yet,' Helen answered.

'We need to think of a plan soon, or it's going to go cold again,' Benjamin said as they both looked into nothingness.

After a moment of silence, Helen spoke with an idea. 'Could we lure them out by pretending the factory is about to Collapse?' Helen mused aloud. Benjamin looked at her, puzzled.

'How do you mean pretend the factory's about to collapse, Helen?'

Taking a moment to properly formulate a plan, Helen replied. 'Well, whoever it was that set Grace's flat alight, did so to either kill me or to get me out. While it didn't kill me, I made every effort to get out of the flat. So, if we do something similar—'

Benjamin interrupted her. 'You think they'll flee out the building, on to the street where we can arrest them?' Benjamin finished Helen's plan.

'Indeed, I do, Benjamin, even Bertie wants to live another day.' At this, they both looked at each other while a sense of warmth filled the room. They stayed there for a moment until a loud bang of the station door being flung open by a newly arrested thief, broke the silence. Helen excused herself and made her way back home. She would wait until Benjamin got back to her with a time and date for when the plan was scheduled.

Chapter 30

As Helen sat at breakfast, it had been a few days since both Benjamin and herself had hatched the plan to lure Bertie and Mary out of their fox hole. Helen knew such a plan would need a lot of personnel, that's not to mention needing permission from the landowner. To successfully pull this off, they may well have to cause damage to the property to convince Bertie that they were in danger. Even then there was no guarantee they would come out; some people would try to hide rather than bolt. What if Bertie saw straight through the plot and not surrender his position?

As per the usual order of events in her day job, the breakfast dishes were packed away, and everyone moved on to morning briefing. The monotony of the day she faced was a harsh reality check for Helen, she couldn't help but feel she wanted to be out on the street, trying to catch Grace's killers. But Helen was to carry on serving the Ellentons. She loved her job. Still, was there something bigger and better out there for her?

She stood in the delivery yard, going over some goods, quality checking them as she usually did, showing to the foreman when they were good to go, and pack the goods away in the kitchen. Helen was so engrossed in her task she didn't notice that Benjamin had come round the corner and was standing, waiting for her to see him.

One foreman coughed loudly; Helen gave him a puzzled look. Have I missed something in the large baskets, Helen thought. 'Someone is waiting for you, ma'am,' the foreman said, moving his head towards where Benjamin was waiting.

Helen followed the foreman's gaze to find Benjamin stood waiting in what had become his usual waiting spot.

'Thank you,' Helen replied to the foreman, as she made her way towards Benjamin, once there she wasted no time in asking for what she hoped he was there for. 'Have we got a date and time yet?' Helen surprised herself at her brisk, harsh tone. Taking a step back from him in her surprise, she hoped Benjamin didn't take it to heart.

Benjamin smiled. 'Yes, Helen, we do, it turns out I know the landowner. I arrested one of his employees for theft, back when I was Detective Arthur's apprentice, so he was more than happy to give us permission to do whatever we need to do to get Bertie and Mary out. Do you think you'll be able to be free a week from now? I still need to get together a team of officers for this plot,' Benjamin asked, still with a boyish grin on his face.

'Yes, Benjamin, I can make that work, what time?' Helen asked.

'It'll be late, as we believe they're staying in the factory overnight, about midnight, that way we know they'll be asleep,' Benjamin answered, a more severe expression covering his face. 'If you are to be there, you must do exactly as I say, they may well target you when they leave the factory. I may be busy with another suspect. If we are to succeed, then I need to know you are safe.' Benjamin's voice was cold and his expression stern, sending chills down Helen's spine.

'Yes, Benjamin, I'll make sure I'm safe.' Helen agreed.

With a nod goodbye, Benjamin turned and walked away. Taking a deep breath, Helen walked back to finish sorting out the delivered goods.

That night, Helen lay in bed rigid and unable to sleep or relax at least, there was something about the conversation with Benjamin that she couldn't escape from. He'd never been that stern with her before. What was he apprehensive about? There would be a team of officers there, ready to make an arrest. What had rattled Benjamin so much?

Helen thought that it may be the fact a lot was riding on this ending successfully in an arrest of at least one suspect, but the stakes were high at the auction and Benjamin was calmer then.

Watching the moonlight disappear behind a cloud through her window, Helen closed her eyes as her need for sleep surrounded her.

She dreamt of how the plan would work, the night sky and the officers waiting around the factory and handcuffs on the wrists of Bertie and Mary. Helen's sense of satisfaction waned as her mind, in its sleepy state, whirled theories about what it was Benjamin was worried about. Helen remembered her attack near the market and details about both fires. Flames and bottle bombs spun around in her head, followed by Benjamin's injuries after her kidnapping. She could hear him call out to her as she tried to avoid the flames to get to him, to get to safety, she felt someone grab her from behind. She woke up with a jolt.

Waking up on the floor, it had all been a bad dream. At least it wasn't real, Helen thought, she was safe, for now.

Getting back into bed, Helen knew she was in for a rough night's sleep as she didn't see the bad dreams going anywhere any time soon. Helen couldn't wait for the time to come where she would be at the factory, she would make sure both Mary and Bertie were caught for what they had done to her, and to Grace.

Nursing her coffee, the following morning, Helen cast her eyes over the paper. There was a mention of the police having a new lead in the murder of the young woman from the Locus Nectar. Helen sighed into her coffee, she thought this could impede their plans to arrest Bertie and Mary.

Reading through the article again, there wasn't any mention what action the police were planning to do or when. The report simply stated that there was a fresh lead and reflected on how long it had taken for the police to find the information, so nothing that would put the plan at risk.

Giving a stern look at Dolly who had been staring at her for a little too long, Helen finished her coffee and gathered her dishes together and piled them in the sink. One of the kitchen staff, eager to make a good impression, had already begun to clean the dishes.

Helen nodded with a sleepy smile on her face, the coffee hadn't kicked in, so there was no verbal praise. The maid seemed a little put off by this but carried on doing the dishes until she was called on to join the crowd that had gathered for the morning briefing.

Helen could barely keep her eyes open; she went about her tasks as she sleepwalked through the week. She counted down the days until it was time for her to be at the factory.

Chapter 31

It was the morning of the day they would try to make a successful arrest of Bertie and Mary. Helen's excitement oozed out of her so much she had to stop what she was doing to either catch her breath or to slow her heart rate down. Between exhaustion and excitement, Helen didn't know whether to sit down and have a coffee when her schedule allowed her to or carry on with her chores to distract herself. Once again having to make a choice about what was important to her at that given point, Helen had to keep appearances up. She had new staff members to train, so couldn't be seen to be slacking off herself.

Looking at her watch, it was twelve noon, she still had eight hours to go until she would need to be at the factory. Helen's heart sank as it was still a full working day away for most people. Sighing, she opted for a cup of tea instead of coffee in her break, there wouldn't be much good in her crashing when she was at the factory when she needed to be most alert and able to move quickly if she needed to move out the way of oncoming danger.

A little while later, Helen watched the sun go down from the kitchen table, soon it'll be time to head towards town. Helen was to meet with Benjamin and the rest of the officers in the station, where Benjamin had set up an investigation room. Cold chills ran down Helen's spine. She wrapped her arms around herself as she made a mental note that she would need to wear her coat out this evening, rather than bring just her shawl.

The time came for Helen to gather all that she would need with her. After she had done so, Helen slipped out into the night. It was about ten o'clock, a little early to set off, but Helen didn't want to be in a rush. She wanted time to prepare herself, the fact that Benjamin worried about this not ending well and for her safety still troubled her.

Helen wondered whether it would be impertinent to ask him what worried him so much. What was the risk that he was warning her about? She had been at risk while solving the case before and yet he'd remained calm. What was different this time?

Walking through town, all was quiet, there was ice in the air. Helen quickened her pace, the night chill tried to seep through her coat as she walked through the streets. As the silence only grew louder, her heartbeat quickened to the point she could hear it in her ears.

Something made her stop dead, her hairs stood on edge, she felt like a deer out in the open, vulnerable to attack. Helen turned to her left and realised she was standing where all this had started. Directly opposite the alley mouth that she had taken only a short while ago, again Helen felt it lure her in. Standing there motionless, she recalled the day she had seen Grace in the alleyway dying a slow and painful death. Her convulsions and her death in the cab with Benjamin and Helen by her side.

Helen knew going back through the alley would be not only reckless but stupid also, so why did she still feel the urge to go through the alley again?

Helen thought about closing her eyes to steady herself, but

her mind couldn't let her. She could feel the adrenaline rising in her as the mouth of the alley seemed to get bigger, then she started to move. Without thinking, she crossed the pavement to the curb. She was cold as ice; she could see her breath in the air as the mist billowed around her.

She lifted her foot to step onto the road, every conscious part of her begging to stop and step back onto the pavement. Helen took another step, and she was now on the road.

As she took her third step into the road, she felt something run across her feet making her jolt back to full consciousness. Looking down, it had been a cat, a street cat, Helen glared at it as it looked at her, a live mouse in its mouth.

Shaking her encounter with the cat off with a shudder, Helen stepped back to the pavement, adamant that she would not be distracted or lured into potentially dangerous situations anymore that evening.

Finally making it to the station, Helen could see Benjamin behind the reception desk, looking up from the ledger he was filling in. He nodded to acknowledge her.

'Helen, meet me in my office, and I'll be there once the other officers have arrived and we'll go through the plan in detail when everybody's here.' Helen nodded back and made her way to his office, sitting in her usual spot and waited for Benjamin to be done filling in the ledger. After a few minutes of just her in his office looking out of the window, Helen heard the door handle twist, turning to face who she thought was Benjamin. It was, in fact, Detective Arthur. Helen noted his attitude towards her hadn't changed as he stood in the corner at the other side of the door to where Helen was sat, never taking his cold glare off her. She thought about making conversation with him, but she didn't want to invite friction between them before going to the factory, that would be the time that they would need to work together, to be a team.

Slowly, other officers piled into the office, making small talk to each other and nodding at Helen. Helen nodded back. Each time Detective Arthur took a deep breath, still uncomfortable with her being there. Shortly after the last officer arrived and people had moved around to make space for everyone, Benjamin came in and made his way through to behind his desk. Once there he looked over everybody and addressed them.

'Right, folks, the people we are about to arrest are connected to the murder case of a young woman called Grace Andrews. I'm sure you're aware, Bertie has avoided arrest both by military law enforcement and ourselves, he is skilled in escape. He has shown to be comfortable in doing whatever is necessary to be free. Mary is not known to us, so we don't know what she'll do when arrested. Be always on your guard, it may be a long one. If we don't catch them now, we will never catch them.' Benjamin paused to make sure all were clear on what he was saying, they could take all force necessary to catch them. Some of the junior officers shuffled uncomfortably, Benjamin looked at them, steadying them slightly and carried on walking them through the plan.

They were to call out to the suspects, bang on the walls and rattle the doors of the old building, smashing the glass with their truncheons if needed, claiming it was about to burn down. At the same time, some other officers would light controlled fires near the building, enough so that if they looked out, they could see the fire but be in no actual danger. Helen was there to alert the officers as to where they had escaped from so that they could make the arrest. Benjamin handed her a whistle.

'I need you to blow on this, and an officer will arrest them. Run after them if necessary but do not engage with them.' Benjamin checked they were all ready and dismissed them into the police vehicles. One was empty where they would hold Bertie and Mary once they were arrested.

Arriving at the factory, everybody dismounted from their vehicles, no one spoke or looked at each other, and they all knew what it was they were to do. Like well-oiled cogs in a machine, some of the officers gathered empty containers to use as a fire pit and piled burnable materials and set them to where Benjamin had said they were to go. Never saying a word, just watching, nodding, and then getting on with the job, the other officers stood in their spots, shifting slightly watching Benjamin for a signal to start the operation.

Looking around, Helen found a spot behind some empty crates that had been slightly covered over. She could be hidden but still see everything that was going on, ready to alert the officers in what direction Mary or Bertie had run in. There was a moment of calm, chilled quiet, all were ready and waiting. Benjamin gave the signal with a strong whistle, and as if an eruption had begun, all officers shouted out, 'Get out, the building is going to burn.'

Helen watched as truncheons were slammed against the old building and the officers lit the fires, letting the flames grow big, bright, and fierce. The officers ran to every side of the building slamming the walls and calling out to Mary and Bertie inside, every few minutes increasing the sense of urgency. Those near the fires added more fuel, this was when they began to rattle the gates, clanking the locks and breaking the glass in the windows. Surely Bertie or Mary will make a break for it.

The tone of the officers turned aggressive, and Helen could see Benjamin begin to pace outside the front door, this indeed was going to be a long one. Just when Helen started to think they had moved on, she heard, above all the noise a large side hatch open. Looking towards the noise, about halfway up the left wall, two figures were beginning to form as they scrambled out of the vent. This was it; it was time for Helen to perform her part in the plot.

She blew the whistle hard, stepping out of her hiding spot and waving frantically. She pointed, using her whole arm to show the officers where they were. She caught sight of Benjamin and two other officers running full pelt her way. Looking back, Bertie and Mary had contacted the ground, Helen took off, still whistling hard as she was told to do.

Keeping a pace that allowed her to be safe but not to lose sight of the two of them, Helen saw Mary trip over something on the ground. Almost in sync, all four of the people who were chasing them sped up, they could catch one.

Helen watched a scene unfold that both baffled her and shed light on the lingering question of the connection between the two suspects. Mary was clearly injured. Still, Bertie merely dismissed her with a wave of his hand.

At this, Mary screamed, 'I did this for us!' Bowing her head, Mary began to sob.

Helen stopped just short of Mary, keeping a close eye on her, whistle in hand, ready for if Mary decided to make a break for it. Mary didn't move. Helen felt a rush of air around her as Benjamin and the two other men, arrested Mary. Looking ahead, Bertie hadn't got past the blockade of fire pits before being arrested.

A sense of jubilation and relief filled the air as both Bertie and Mary were loaded into the second vehicle. The fires were put out, barrels put back where they were, and everyone piled back into the first vehicle. It was a job well done.

Once at the station, Helen watched as Benjamin and another senior officer clambered down the stairs with Bertie and Mary in handcuffs. She knew she needed to leave shortly, and Helen didn't need to be there anymore. She had done what she had set out to do and had won. Setting the whistle down on Benjamin's desk, she paused for a moment looking at the case bored. She wondered if she should begin to unpin them and set them in a pile on his desk for him but thought better of it as it was evidence, it was up to Benjamin to file away and close the case. Helen made her way out of the office and towards the front door, sliding past the hub of officers logging out, making sure they were paid their overtime. Helen opened the door just as Benjamin ascended the stairs. She smiled, and he nodded goodnight.